A HUNTER'S FATE

A SUPERNATURAL PROVINCE NOVEL

B. K. RAE

First paperback edition 2019

Published by Sophisticated Magic, LLC

Editing by Watch Jane Write

Cover Design by Justin Shafer

Proofreading by Roseann M. Karnes & Watch Jane Write

Paperbook and eBook Interior Formatting by The Illustrated Author Design Services
(www.theillustratedauthor.net)

Paperback ISBN: 9781089785743

This is a work of fiction. Names, characters, places, and incidents which are used are the product of the author's imagination or are used factiously. Any resemblance to actual persons, living or dead, events, or locales is entirely coincidental.

Warning

This book is intended for mature audiences and contains violence, explicit language, and sexual activity.

Trademarks Used

Mustang © Ford Motor Company, **Jameson** © Irish Distillers Limited,
Nike © Nike, Inc., **Dodge Ram** © FCA US LLC,
Doc Martens © AIRWAIR INTL. LTD, **Escalade** © General Motors,
Vogue © Condé Nast., **Mike Tyson** © Mike Tyson, **Chuck Taylor** © Converse

Thank you to all who encouraged me along the way. Without you, this would not have been possible.

PRELUDE

The sounds of my feet hammering against the grated iron of the old warehouse echoed through the unnaturally silent June evening. Between my attempt to flee and my ragged breathing, the sounds reverberated in the abandoned building, causing a tumultuous effort to remain concealed.

Right, left, right, left, right, left.

My mind raced, trying to contemplate an escape route that would lead me out of this alive.

At the academy, we learned to act skillfully in high-pressure situations. Hesitation for even one second could be the difference between life or death, so every moment mattered. The lectures of my instructors rolled through my mind as I determined the best course of action. Until I came up with a plan, I did the one thing I could do to buy some time; I ran. Thankfully, scheming happened to be a strength of mine. Running, not so much.

I continued down the metal grating, trying to remain in the shadows of the archaic stone building. Attempting to seek a way out while remaining on guard proved more difficult than I anticipated, and I felt my energy waning.

I stopped just short of a passageway that led to the first-floor landing. Using this reprieve, I rested my hands on my knees, taking deep breaths as I steadied my thoughts and erratic heart. As I scanned the first floor, I spotted a door leading to the outside. If it weren't for the glow of the moon shining through the broken window, I would have never seen it as darkness enveloped the entire building. *Oh, thank you, sweet baby Jesus.* I just needed to push a little further. The crunch of glass under the boots of those that ran toward me energized my attempts to escape, and I took off once more. I heard them closing in.

Normally in places like this, it's easy to hide and lie low because there were so many nooks and crannies. But, leave it to me to find the most open floor plan in existence. There was also the fact I was set up, cornered, and deceived. I was alone.

Ugh, I really needed to start telling people where I was going.

That seemed to be a problem of mine—acting before I thought. I prayed to whoever was listening that if I made it out of this, I'd work on it. Continuing my sprint, I made it to the bottom of the stairs and onto the landing of the open floor. Even though I reached the ground level, I still had aways to go until I met my escape. I slid into the shadows beneath the stairs, inhaling a deep breath to settle and let my mind assess what to do next. I needed to evaluate where they were and how many remained, and I needed to execute a plan because one wrong move and I wouldn't survive.

Closing my eyes, I utilized my enhanced hearing to sort through the different sounds of the warehouse. I counted a total of four of them. Judging by the rate they moved, they were strong, fast, and determined. I shuddered. *Vampires.* This wasn't an accident, I was the bait all along, and at this realization, panic set in. I needed to go, and I needed to go now. As I dashed toward the exit, I stopped in my tracks when a vampire stood directly above me. He must have sensed that I was close because he paused and slowly sniffed the air, causing me to cringe.

He continued down the stairs in my direction, but with my stealth and speed, he never saw me coming. He rounded the corner, and my fist connected with his face. The force of my blow rippled through his entire body, making him stumble back against the railing. Disoriented, he swung around, determined to find what hit him. But once again, I was too quick. I landed another blow to his chest. He hunched over in pain, which gave me the opportunity to encircle his neck and render him useless in one swift crack. I recoiled at the sound of the aggressive act, but when it came to him or me, I chose me.

I slipped him under the stairs to avoid further detection and checked his form for any weapons that I could use, pulling a single pocket knife out of his jacket. *That's it?* I wondered. I gripped the blade in my hand as my head snapped up, hearing the others gaining ground. As the other vampires made their way to me, it was time to make a break for it. I ran like my life depended on it, which it did.

"She's heading toward the door!" one of them yelled, giving away any disguise the darkness gave me.

I took off as fast as my legs would take me in hopes of getting to the door unscathed. My mind was in overdrive, and it felt like my heart was going to beat out of my chest. I could hear two of them coming down the stairs, and with one last look over my shoulder, one of the vampires was ripped into the shadows as a scream sounded. There was a gurgle, then silence as a growl emanated from the same area. His partner didn't seem to register the attack of his companion and continued toward me. He was too quick. He would get to me before I would reach the door. Turning to stand my ground and fight, an enormous brown wolf stalked its way toward the vampire. I observed in stunned silence as the wolf leaped onto the back of the vampire, and he howled in pain, trying to roll the beast off of him. I was grateful for the wolf; however, I wasn't about to stand around to see what happened.

I continued my way to the door, my path now completely open. I pushed my legs harder than ever as there were only a few feet until freedom. I was almost to the door of the warehouse when someone

Perdón

blocked my exit. Realization hit me hard; I had forgotten there was one more vampire in the building—only it wasn't a vampire. Taking in the form in front of me, I froze in place. It was then that I recognized who was before me. Relief washed over me at the thought of someone here to help.

"What are you doing here?" I asked in my panicked state. "It doesn't matter." I shook it off. "We have to go, now."

Only he wasn't moving. He made his way inside the warehouse, essentially boxing me in with the vampire that currently fought behind me. Comprehension dawned on me as to what happened, and my blood turned cold. He wasn't here to help me; he was the one chasing me. He was the one who set me up. Betrayal flooded through my system.

As if he registered my thoughts, he held up Reed's phone as a sinister smile crept across his lips. I was appalled.

"You son of a bitch!" I shouted, echoing the betrayal I felt.

"Sorry, darling," he replied as I heard another crunch behind me.

I involuntarily turned toward the sound. It was just a second, but it was almost a lethal mistake. Realizing what I had done, I turned back around quickly, only to be met with an exploding pain in my temple, and a second blow came just as quickly, rendering me useless. The unbearable pain caused me to fall to the ground. I tried to get back up to defend myself, only my limbs were not cooperating.

This is it. This is how you're going to die. Of all the stupid shit you've done, this is how it's going to end? As I tried once more to balance myself on my knees and gather my bearings, he stalked me with a look of smug contentment on his face. He clenched and unclenched his fists, ready to provide another blow. Blackness threatened my vision, and it was only when I was on the brink of nothingness that enraged snarling reverberated behind me. Both of us froze as the wolf approached, only he wasn't heading toward me, he was rushing *him.*

My vision blurred again as I felt the warmth of my blood slip over my temple. I tried to keep my eyes open, only no matter how much I willed them, my attempts remained unsuccessful. I risked another attempt to stand, but my legs gave out, and I landed on all fours. After a few minutes, I realized the sounds of fighting and growling ceased. I heard heavy footsteps retreating out of the warehouse. Judging by the shadow on the retreating form, my traitor was fleeing.

"Yeah, you better fucking run!" I yelled, my voice sounding raspy. My words slurred from the major concussion I was sure I had received. At my words, the most beautiful, rich, chuckle echoed in the air. The sound was smoother than silk. I looked up to see the source of the laughter and was met with a tall, broad figure walking to me. As I was about to get into a defensive position and push into a stand, the most beautiful set of luminous, green eyes came into view, staring directly into my soul. *Is he real? Um, is he not wearing a shirt?* I couldn't tell if the creature in front of me was a product of a hallucination from my head injury; not to mention, he was so stunning he must have been imagined. But at that moment, it dawned on me. I knew that face. The club, those eyes, the electric touch.

"You," was all I managed to get out as I felt the blackness take over.

"It's okay, I'm not going to hurt you," he replied. He held both hands up, palms facing me.

I was on the brink of consciousness and collapsed to my knees once again when a pair of warm, strong arms wrapped around me. Before the blackness took over, one final thought flashed through my mind. *How the hell do I always end up in these situations?*

I guess I better start from the beginning.

ONE

HENNY
36 hours earlier

"What you did was unbelievably reckless! Did you even think of the consequences had things not turned out the way they did?" Demetri's eyes burned with rage as he glared down at me from the desk he sat behind. His jaw ticked, and it looked as if the vein in his forehead would burst. Directly behind Demetri stood Gareth, with his hands clasped behind his back and a look of disappointment on his face. He was smart enough to keep quiet. "You never think! You always act on—"

"Listen," I said rising to my feet. My heart rate increased, a product of anger and the need to defend my actions. I narrowed my eyes in his direction.

I heard Daxon curse at my outburst. My brother stood behind me, his arms crossed over his chest. His foot rested against the wall, so his knee stuck out. I couldn't believe I was getting reprimanded for my performance. It was because I was a woman. If this were Gareth or Dax, they would be hailed as a hero.

"Everyone got out, didn't they?" I expressed an attitude that matched Demetri's in anger and tone. "We got the intel we needed, and

6

we probably even saved a few lives while we were at it. Had we sat on our asses like a few wanted to, we probably wouldn't have gotten what we did. It's not my fault that some of your lazy ass—"

"ENOUGH!" Demetri screamed, rising to his feet as his face turned an aggressive shade of scarlet.

"What is going on in here?" a voice floated from the door into the office we all currently resided in. Relief flooded through me as all eyes locked onto my father, who now occupied the doorway.

Demetri's demeanor immediately changed, and his body language deflated. "Sir, there were a few issues with the mission today," Demetri stated more calmly than when he had spoken to me.

My father's eyes met mine with a glint of humor in them. *He knew me too well.*

Demetri continued. "Proper protocol was not followed, and rules were broken that could have led to causalities."

"What happened?" my father responded by questioning the tension of the situation. When no one answered, he continued. "I thought we retrieved the information on the vampires and not only discovered, but saved, four human girls that were under compulsions and held captive, did we not?"

Demetri looked thwarted at the turn of the conversation and tried to reconcile the issue further. "Yes, sir, but—" he stammered, but my father cut him off.

"I will take care of this. You are relieved. Thank you," he commanded from his spot with a nod. As Demetri stalked off, my father stopped him before he reached the doorway. "Demetri, if I ever hear you take that tone with my daughter again, there will be consequences. That's not how we handle our business."

With a tight nod, Demetri hurried out the door, leaving my dad to deal with Gareth, Daxon, and I.

My father walked into the office, taking residence behind the dark oak desk. I sat back down in one of the chairs in front of him, letting out a long sigh. My father folded his hands in his lap, staring at me as

I squirmed under his gaze. My hand flew to the diamond pendant I've worn since I was a child. One of the earliest memories I have from my childhood was the day my father gave it to me. Dad explained that it was my mother's, and it was very near and dear to her. I remember how proud I felt that he had given me something so special to protect. I haven't taken it off since that day. Playing with the chain was a nervous habit of mine; running my fingers along the necklace was almost therapeutic as it made me feel close to her.

The commanding presence of Jonah Bradford was a little intimidating. The power and leadership that radiated off him didn't go unnoticed by anyone, which wasn't surprising given the title he held.

My father was one of four executive guardians that oversaw the Southern Province of Supernatural Hunters. My sect of hunters commanded unidentified activity as far north as Tennessee and as far west as Texas. We also inspected everything on the southeastern coasts and the Gulf of Mexico. Those were the missions I yearned for. There was nothing I loved more than enjoying the beautiful ocean sun. Typically, we didn't have to travel very often as my father was able to delegate to different provinces in our region, so we usually stayed in our hometown of good ole' New Orleans, Louisiana.

My father was respected, valued, and one of the most prominent leaders in the supernatural realm, which is why his disappointing gaze caused me so much unrest. He sat with his eyebrows raised as if anticipating an explanation. I looked between Daxon and Gareth, only to find their gazes glued to the floor. *Cowards.*

I tried to think of an explanation, but I was distracted by the nostalgia of the room. The sun shone through the stained-glass windows, and the most beautiful colors radiated off the floor next to my father as well as over the bookshelves. This room was one of my favorite places in the manor, except when I was in trouble. More times than I could count, I would sneak in here at all hours of the night to sit on the windowsill, reading all things supernatural.

My father cleared his throat, waiting for an explanation; however, it was Gareth who spoke first.

"Henny, I don't know why you provoke him, you're going to give him a heart attack," Gareth stated as he came around from behind the desk and sat in the chair next to me. We locked eyes, and I registered the disappointment in them. I did hate upsetting him. Gareth was one of my oldest friends. Gareth, Daxon, Reed, and I had been extremely close over the years, and it hurt to see the disappointment laced in his stare.

"Actually, it was kind of funny," Daxon stated as he approached the desk from the corner of the room. Daxon, my twin brother, was a mirror image of me, only in the male version. His rumpled blonde hair and blue eyes matched mine perfectly. Although we looked alike, he towered over me by a foot. Daxon was tall and strong, his lean figure making him the most agile of us all, and his experience in fighting made him one of our most trusted hunters. He harbored one weakness, though—he was almost as cocky about his abilities as I was. Almost.

"Enough, Daxon," my father shot back at him, seemingly annoyed by the situation while rolling his eyes. "Henny, what you did today was completely against protocol. Going in on your own without reporting it to anyone first? It could have been dangerous for a number of reasons. The information that we received may have been inaccurate, and you could have walked right into a trap. There is also the fact that backup may not have gotten there in time, and you could have been severely injured. What if they would have captured you? Do I need to keep going? Commands not being followed leads to signals getting crossed. Someone could have really gotten hurt. Do you understand? What you did today was reported to me by no less than three hunters."

I shook my head, hating the public shaming I received, but he was right, it could have been a lot it worse. Jonah could have harbored a lot more anger. As the adrenaline from the raid this afternoon finally wore off, I contemplated my actions. I was sympathetic that it didn't go as planned.

"I'm sorry," I responded as I blew out a long breath.

"Are you, Henrietta?" my father questioned.

I remained silent and fidgety under his irritated stare. I hated when he used my full name. Most people knew better than to use it. If it weren't for my mother, who had picked it out, I would have changed it. Thankfully, most everyone stuck to Henny.

"What is our motto?" he asked.

"Think first, act later," the three of us responded at the same time.

He eventually smiled, and I felt the small breath I held escape from my lungs. My father's eyes landed on me once again. "You are so much like your mother. I should have known you would be just like her. Defiant, but strong. Loyal—to a fault," he said while staring at the oak desk, reminiscing as he got that far off look in his eye—the way he always did when he thought about her.

My mother died shortly after childbirth, and it appeared that even after twenty-two years, my father was still undeniably in love with her. To this day, I have never seen him with another woman. My father stood from behind the desk and addressed all three of us, carrying a proud stance. If there was one thing my father excelled at, it was being an excellent leader.

"Even after the mishap we had today," he said, looking at me and winking. "I'm extremely proud of all of you. What you did today, you guys are making a difference," he finished as satisfaction radiated off him—a proud father beaming at his children's accomplishments. Even though Daxon and I were his only biological children, Gareth might as well be as my father took him in at the age of two when his parents died. The Frederiksen's were close friends of my father's, so he instantly took Gareth in, and he's been with us ever since. Not to mention, with short, blond hair and brown eyes, he sometimes looked more like Daxon's twin than me as they were the same height.

"Why don't you guys get some rest this weekend, and we'll pick back up on Monday? We received some good intel, and it will take a day or two to sort through it. After that, there are some regions and new protocols I want to go over."

Gareth and Daxon, still in hunter mode, nodded understanding and stood as they waited to be dismissed. I, however, bounced over to my father and gave him a quick peck on the cheek.

"Love you, Dad," I said, trying to lay on the charm. If there was one thing he had a weakness for, it was his Bradford women.

"Love you too, Pumpkin," my father responded.

Daxon and Gareth nodded goodbye as we made our way out of his study. Sauntering down the glass-paneled hallway, we saw the hunters in the courtyard practicing. Daxon stopped and turned, almost running right into me.

"What?" he said with his eyebrows raised. I feigned innocence. Rolling his eyes, he continued. "Even after just getting in trouble, I can practically feel you scheming from here," he stated, and I smiled. *Freaky twin thing.*

"Well," I eyed him. "Ironically, it's Reed's birthday, and we have just been granted two days of freedom. That is forty-eight hours of unadulterated fun, so I'm thinking I have a date with my best friends and some Long Islands," I said with a wink. Judging by the way my brother froze at my comment, he had forgotten it was Reed's birthday.

Reed was my longtime best friend and secretly my brother's first, and only, love. Reed and I met each other when Jake Baker pulled Vanessa's hair on the playground on our first day at the academy. Reed and I both pushed him down and told him to never mess with any of us ever again. That's all it took, instant best friends. Vanessa, who we called Nessa for short, came over to say thanks. We've all been close ever since.

As if I watched the scene unwinding from afar, it was there on the playground that Daxon fell in love with the red-headed girl. Though neither of them will admit it, they both have strong feelings for each other. They both deny it any time I try to bring it up. I think it has something to do with being worried about how I'll respond or because they both think the other doesn't have feelings for them. Honestly, it couldn't have happened to better people. My two favorite people.

My eyes twinkled when I looked at Daxon, and I realized, judging by the look in his eyes, he did, in fact, forget it was Reed's birthday.

"Well, Romeo, since you forgot it was our best friend's birthday, I suggest you use your newfound spare time to get her a present. That is, if you don't want to deal with the wrath of Reed McGowan for forgetting her birthday, again," I proposed as Daxon looked back at me nervously. "Man, it's a good thing I left a list of gifts she'd like on the desk inside your room," I stated, and Daxon beamed.

"You're the best, Hen," he smiled as he took off out the door, leaving me standing in the stone hallway alone with Gareth.

I had almost forgotten he was there. Gareth looked at me the way he always did, like he was going to use this alone time to lecture me on safety. I knew the tips and tricks; I just actively avoided them. I knew what was coming.

"I really wish that you would be more careful, Henny. What happened today could have gone terribly wrong, I don't know what I would have done—" but he stopped himself and stepped back, putting his hands in his pockets.

Wait, what was happening? I took a step back. "Gareth, I appreciate your concern. But, I was more than capable of taking care of myself today and will be moving forward. I've always been able to take care of myself."

"I know," he replied as he looked down at his shoes for a few minutes and then looked back up at me.

Was this more awkward than normal? Was it always this awkward? Before he said anything else, I broke the silence. "Well, I'm going to grab Reed and get everything ready for tonight. Enjoy your evening," I stated curtly and left before he had a chance to respond.

Practically skipping down the halls of the manor, I took in the beauty of the building on this sunny day. The sun was sparkling off the white columns onto the outside balcony as fellow hunters sat outdoors discussing lessons or trading stories from the night before. Being in Louisiana, the academy already had an old plantation feel to it, but the vines that slithered up the outside of the manor gave it an even bigger southern vibe. Acting as the academy for our province, there was never a shortage of hunters, and no matter where I turned, someone was greeting me as I passed by. Bouncing up three flights of stairs, I made my way to the red and orange entry at the end of the hallway, my favorite door. I bounded right in. Reed and Nessa lounged on Reed's hot pink bed reading magazines. Both straightened upon my arrival. Reed looked up at me with concern as she anticipated the major trouble I was in.

With pale skin and bright red hair, Reed's startling blue eyes looked even more blue than usual when they were masked with concern. Looking the complete opposite with a calm temperament, brown-haired and brown-eyed Nessa was much more relaxed but still relieved to see me.

"So, what happened?" Reed was the first to ask, and I smiled.

"It's okay, everything is fine," I responded, and both of my friends visibly relaxed.

"Meaning she sweet talked Jonah, again," Nessa retorted with a chuckle as we all laughed.

Unfortunately, due to my personality of recklessness and fearlessness, anxiety was a constant expression on my best friend's face.

"Even though everything is okay, there is a vital matter to attend to," I spoke as my tone grew very serious. "It's of the utmost importance, and we need to rectify it immediately."

Reed and Nessa perked back up as if something was wrong, and Reed stood up to walk over to me. "What is it?" she questioned, the anxiety back on her face.

I giggled and threw a pillow at her. "Where are we going for your birthday tonight?!"

TWO

COLE

Damn, it was hot out. Even for early June, it was hotter than normal in New Orleans. I wiped my forehead with the back of my hand as I was sitting at the wrought iron table outside of the tiny café, the heat of the sun bearing down upon me. I glanced back to the magazine that I was pretending to read, only I wasn't reading, I was watching and waiting.

A lot has been changing recently, and my family and I were trying to gain insight as to what the hell was happening in the supernatural society, hence why I was here at this exact moment. Silent unrest was occurring, and as my family and I were a part of the supernatural community, we wanted to know what was going on.

I thought about the information Liam had passed along and looked at the text message he sent me one more time. This is where she would be, based on her schedule for the day. She always came to this location at this time of day for her caffeine fix. She had for the past month, at least. Tapping my fingers on the table, I was getting a little unsettled. I really didn't want to be here. But, "sometimes you have to do what you have to do." Liam's voice said as it was echoing through my mind. Along with the text, I glanced at her picture again.

Liam had asked me to follow Henrietta Bradford, who was practically hunter royalty. The Bradford clan had justly ruled and fairly governed the supernatural in this area; lately though, there had been whispers that some of the hunters were taking more drastic measures and throwing down harsher punishments to supernatural creatures. My family and I were most concerned about the treatment of the werewolves, which I just happened to be.

I was a member of a small pack that resided in the outskirts of New Orleans. We mostly kept to ourselves as the pack consisted of my two brothers, our sister, and me. From time to time, there would be others who were seeking momentary refuge, and we would help them out. But mostly, it was just us. And I liked it that way. The fewer people I had to deal with, the better.

We were used to being on our own. Our parents had passed away a few years ago after a vampire attack gone wrong. To this day, we still don't know what happened, only that hunters and vampires were involved, which is why we were always watching both groups closely. At least I did, anyway. I was certain that one of those two groups were the reason my parents were gone. It had been hard without them, they were the core of our family.

When my parents were alive, my father, who was Alpha at the time, was always speaking of werewolf tradition and the importance of pack life. He would direct the conversation to all of us, but we all knew he was guiding Liam, my oldest brother. Liam was the ideal wolf to take over our pack when our father stepped down. Being his Beta, Liam was a strategic thinker; a true leader and he knew how to make the right decision when it was called for. My brothers and I were close in age, each of us only being a year apart, which made us a close-knit pack. I was the youngest brother, having turned twenty-four last month.

We were all shocked when my father passed, and the Alpha mark had not been passed on to Liam but was transferred to me. The morning after my parents had died, I had awoken from endless hours of tossing and turning, only to find the Alpha mark of our pack painted on my rib cage, under my left arm. I couldn't wrap my head around why it had occurred, and I sure as hell didn't want to be Alpha. Liam was better suited for it. Frustration and resentment at this newfound responsibility was crushing me.

Liam, being the loyal brother that he was, recognized me as the Alpha and was guiding me through the process. It was evident that he would be my Beta. As the Beta, Liam and I had the closest relationship when in our wolf forms. The connection was only secondary to a mate connection. I knew that it bothered him that he wasn't chosen. Hell, it bothered me. Liam should have been Alpha. So why was it me?

Lost in thoughts of my family, I didn't realize a black Escalade was approaching the curb. Once it came to a stop, I slumped in my chair a little further and picked up a magazine, so I wouldn't be as easy to spot. It was only then that I noticed I had picked up the latest issue of Vogue. I cursed under my breath at the discovery, and the older lady that was sitting at the next table grinned at me.

To the normal eye, you couldn't tell that we were werewolves unless we shifted right in front of you; however, that still didn't mean I was wanting to draw any attention to myself. I gave her a curt nod and turned back around.

After the Escalade rolled to a stop, the driver came around to the back of the vehicle to open the rear door, only to be waved off by the person who was exiting the car. When I took notice of who was stepping out, I stopped breathing.

When Liam sent me the information on Henrietta Bradford, the picture that was painted made Henrietta look like a sweet, quiet girl. Obviously, she was a hunter, so she was skilled, but at five-foot-nothing and one-hundred-and-fifteen pounds, she seemed delicate, like someone who was not out fighting supernatural creatures. The Henrietta that stepped out of the back of that SUV was not the Henrietta that I had grown accustomed to from the written information.

You could tell instantly that the woman who had stepped out would take control of a room and a situation. As she left the Escalade, her back instantly straightened, and her posture screamed vixen. Raking my eyes up her beautiful body, I took in her black stilettos and her dark blue skinny jeans, which were practically painted onto her perfectly firm legs and amazingly sculpted ass.

Though she was thin, she had the most luscious hips, and the black corset she was wearing accentuated her cleavage, drawing attention to her long neck. I couldn't even begin to imagine how good it would feel to put my lips on her perfectly smooth skin. *What the hell?* I checked myself at the thought, but I couldn't help but notice the blonde curls that were cascading down to the middle of her back. Her eyes were hidden by a pair of dark-mirrored aviators, which made her bronze skin look even more attractive. *Fuck, she was sexy.* I couldn't take my eyes off her, along with every other male within a three-block radius.

She was walking up to the entrance of the café and flashed a sexy, sly smile to the teenage boy who was opening the door for her with his mouth agape. Her beauty was so distracting that the poor kid didn't stand a chance, no man would. The boxes he was working to stack went tumbling to the ground. Henrietta had bent down to help him, but he waved her away, flushed with embarrassment as his cheeks turned scarlet. I cocked my head as I took in her bent form, holding in a whistle that was threatening to escape from my lips. It was no wonder that Liam didn't want Bran, my other brother, to take this detail. He would have been all over her in an instant.

Once the shock of her attractiveness wore off, I remembered that Liam had said she normally spent about twenty minutes inside and then would leave. The entire time I was waiting for her to exit, I hadn't stop thinking about her legs, her hips, her chest. Shaking off the memory, I had to remember the reason I was here, a lot was happening in our world, and it may be the hunters who were at the cause of it. I needed to remain indifferent.

I tried to use my enhanced hearing to get a hint on what was happening inside the café, to determine if she was meeting with anyone. However, I was met with complete silence. Either the café was soundproofed, or it was charmed so no one could hear what was going on inside. *Sneaky hunters.*

Almost twenty minutes on the dot, Henrietta was walking out of the shop with someone following her. She was accompanied by another young girl around our age who was not as gorgeous as Henrietta, but still pretty. I couldn't control my eyes following Henrietta's fluid movements wherever she went. The two girls appeared to have a causal relationship, and Henrietta was asking her fellow hunter if she had any plans for later.

This peaked my interest, and I listened more closely to see if anything was discussed. Henrietta responded that they were going to Fuze for Reed's birthday. *Reed McGowan, the best friend.* The girl excitedly agreed to join, and Henrietta seemed happy with her choice. After a quick hug, the two shared goodbyes and parted ways as Henrietta got into the Escalade, which then headed south on Main Street.

I sat and contemplated the information for a while, the shock of her beauty was still rippling through my system. There was one thing I knew. I needed to see more of her. I pulled out my phone and called my brother, Bran. When he answered on the first ring, I asked him one question.

"Are you still looking for something to do tonight?"

THREE

HENNY

After hours of primping, curling, makeup, and wine; Nessa, Reed, and I were ready to go out. I needed this. After the tense mission this afternoon and the scolding after, I craved relaxation. Heading out for a few drinks with Reed and Nessa was just what I needed to rectify that.

Reed wore a hunter-green high-neck dress which accentuated her long, red curls. The color looked gorgeous against her fair skin and made her blue eyes burst with beauty. Nessa wore a magenta halter-top dress and matching heels with her hair swept into the most elegant up-do. In another life, Nessa would be a personal stylist to the celebrities. She loved doing it, which was perfect for me because I didn't know how to do anything other than rock a ponytail. Mostly side ponytails. Everyone Nessa touched and styled looked like they were featured in a magazine, so I was happy to oblige when she offered to do our hair and makeup.

Feeling a little feisty, I wore a soft but tight fire-engine-red, strapless dress with ruching at the sides and a mid-thigh length. I definitely needed to get out of the manor before my father saw it. I donned black heels and threw on some red lipstick for another layer of sassiness. I admired my hair that Nessa styled into a waterfall braid hanging loosely over my left shoulder. As hunters, we didn't get out much, so we made a statement tonight.

We decided to keep to ourselves while we got ready. If my dad caught wind of what we were doing, he would surely try to put an end to it. It would be considered too dangerous, especially after the events this afternoon. But, the nature of our work made danger increase on a daily basis, and it was a cruel reality that we might not make it to our next birthday. We always celebrated these days to the fullest when they came around. Go big or go home.

Knowing that Dax, Gareth, and my father were in a strategy meeting with the inner circle of the hunters, the three of us made our way down the stairs to the main entryway. Jared, a sixteen-year-old new recruit, guarded the entrance. *This was too easy.* He eyed us apprehensively as we made our way toward him.

"Jared, how are you doing this evening?" I said, sweetly laying on the charm.

He seemed nervous to be around the three of us. Smart man. We were small, petite women, but we intimidated the hell out of people. We were the most renowned hunters, not to mention part-time instructors at the academy.

"Just fine, thank you," he responded curtly, clearly uncomfortable but not wanting to appear rude, knowing my status in the hunter realm.

"Slow night?" I responded back at him, knowing that the younger recruits had an easy night after the more experienced hunters would most likely spend the evening recovering.

"Yes, but you already know that," he looked around nervously like he would get in trouble talking to us. *He knows what is coming.* I batted my eyelashes a little more than necessary.

"We're going to need a ride into town. You don't have to worry about giving us a ride home, we will find our way back."

"Ah, Henny, come on. You know that I'm not supposed to let anyone leave while everyone is de-briefing. Not to mention the fact that I would be leaving my post. Gareth will have my ass when he finds out I have taken you guys."

I contemplate what he said for a minute and almost, *almost*, felt bad. "You let me worry about Gareth. If he says anything to you, I'll take care of it. Now, you can either drive us into town while they are still in the meeting and be gone for ten minutes, or you can explain to the seniors why an Escalade is missing when they do their evening inventory once the meeting is done. Either way, we're going into town." All three sets of our eyes were on Jared. Reed even threw her hands on her hips.

"Jared, you were interested in getting into my father's defenses seminar next semester, correct?" I countered, and his eyes narrowed. I knew I had him.

"Fine, let's go. But make it quick, I have to get back soon." Smiling and winking at my friends, we were on our way.

Reed beamed, she needed this as much as I did. I was glad that she was excited. I knew she felt guilty about how Daxon would feel that we went out behind their backs, but he would be fine—this was originally his idea. Not to mention it didn't matter, my brother's world began and ended with Reed, both of them were just too blind to see it. He would be alright with whatever she did, as long as it kept her safe and made her happy. Gareth and my father would be a problem, but they would be much more fun to deal with after I had a few drinks in me.

When we pulled up to Fuze, the place was absolutely packed. I thanked Jared again for the ride and assured him we would be fine. Nessa and Reed were already bounding out the door and practically sprinted to get inside. As I stepped out of the vehicle, I felt a warm, tingling sensation creep down the back of my neck, which halted me in place. I glanced around; however, nothing seemed out of the ordinary. *Weird.* This has never happened before. There were hundreds of people walking around The Quarter and waiting in line to enter the club so it could be anything. I needed to be vigilant. Only, the further I walked, the warmer the sensation became as it floated from my head to toes, almost like a soft caress. I glanced around again. I instantly appreciated the fact that I hid an academy-issued dagger in the thigh holster under my dress. I sent a silent prayer I wouldn't need to use it tonight.

Finally moving forward, I acknowledged the bouncer and made my way to the entrance to meet Nessa and Reed. As a fellow hunter owned the club, we were admitted immediately, much to the distaste of the patrons waiting outside the building.

Walking into Fuze, there was definitely a modern and hip atmosphere. The place seemed to be flooded with individuals who were around the same age as us. Low and dim lighting brought attention to the neon designs that radiated off the floor and ceiling, while neon pinks and greens adorned the light fixtures on the wall in a circular pattern. The dance floor was packed, and the DJ pumped techno music through the speakers. I felt the bass reverberating in my chest. Apparently, everyone thought this was the place to be tonight.

The girls and I made our way up to the second floor VIP section that was typically reserved for hunters. I knew there would be a high-top table overlooking the dance floor reserved for us. We passed the hunter bartender, and I flashed him a smile, signaling to get us a round of drinks. He returned my smile with a wink as he pulled out three glasses to get started on our cocktails. Reed made her way to the table, sitting down and relaxing instantly. The life of a hunter wasn't easy, neither was being my best friend. She deserved this; she deserved a night to let loose for a bit. I would give her that much.

Nessa and I took our seats as we waited for our drinks. Looking over the balcony onto the dance floor, the tingling sensation returned, setting me further on edge. I looked more intently into the crowd to see if I noticed anything. As darkness shadowed the dance floor, I could only make out the outlines of the individuals that danced to the music. My relaxing night with my girlfriends was vanishing before my eyes, and I made a silent curse at the sensation.

I distinctly felt someone watching us, an unknown presence hidden in the shadows. The only other person who knew we were here was Jared, and he knew not to tell anyone. He would get in just as much trouble as us if they found out he drove. Daxon knew we were going out, but like the loyal brother he was, he wouldn't have said anything. Gareth was ruled out, too, as he was most likely still debriefing. My spine stood at attention in my seat.

"What's wrong?" Reed asked when her face turned from me and looked out onto the dance floor.

"Nothing," I responded as I checked myself with a smile, not wanting Reed to think anything was off. As I reassured her that we were fine, the bartender arrived with our drinks.

"And what are you three gorgeous ladies up to this evening?" he asked.

I flashed him a charming smile. "It's my best friend's birthday tonight, so keep the drinks flowing."

He returned the charm with a stunning grin. Nessa and Reed both looked like they would melt on the spot.

"Happy Birthday, Reed. You look stunning," he said as he took the top of her hand and gave it a feather-light kiss. Then he sauntered his way back toward the bar.

"Oh my God, Henny, he is so hot! What about him? I bet he would be a welcoming challenge," Nessa responded as I caught onto her hidden meaning. Reed giggled beside her and openly agreed.

"Excuse me, bartender, can you help Henny find the rest of her dress? She appears to have lost it," Reed retorted as I wadded up a napkin and threw it at her. They always tried setting me up.

"Would you guys just stop?" I responded. "I can't take you anywhere," I said as we all sipped our drinks.

It was easy for them to talk about hooking up with guys. Nessa was already mated to Tate and Reed was well on her way to mating Daxon, if they ever got together. That left me the only one without a potential mate, which was fine with me. I didn't need to be tied down. Serious and relationship were two words that were not in my vocabulary. My dad thought otherwise.

As hunters, mates were more than just lovers. We were partners, set to enrich one another's strengths while balancing each other's weaknesses. Mates were often completely compatible and the perfect companions. They were also our biggest allies in battles. Honestly, I wasn't sure if anyone would ever be compatible with my compulsive nature. This thought made me take a long pull of my drink.

"Okay," I declared. "A toast. Happy Birthday to my best friend, may our friendship always be stronger than our drinks. Thank you for being you," I said as Reed's eyes sparkled at the remarks.

"Cheers!" we all exclaimed and drank in her honor.

The evening passed fairly quickly, and I was losing the edge I felt from the tingling sensations earlier. More drinks came as different guys flocked to our table, attempting to win one of us over. They tried to talk to us, but I had to dismiss them away as both Nessa and Reed were too sweet to do so. The bartender had been a godsend with our drinks and kept them flowing all night. Putting the last round of shots down, the bartender announced they were on the house, giving me another sly wink as he walked away. The girls, once again, encouraged me to go after him. He was super attractive, but what the girls didn't realize was that he was probably more interested in Daxon than Reed was. After I took the shot, I stood up, needing to dance off some of this tension.

"Let's go, bitches. I know we didn't get all dressed up to sit on our asses and not show the world how good we look," I said with a little shimmy.

Both of their eyes lit up and they squealed with satisfaction as we made our way downstairs to the dance floor. It was a little after eleven o'clock, and the place was packed to capacity.

Dancing for a while was the perfect reprieve, and I finally felt relaxed. I watched Reed and Nessa while Reed attempted the robot, making all of us laugh. All the drinks I had caught up to me, and I announced to my friends that I was going to the bathroom.

Once I used the restroom, I took a quick look in the mirror and reapplied a coat of lipstick before making my way back to the dance floor. Walking down the darkened hallway, a guy, that looked to be around my age, made his way toward me. Even though he was shadowed, I could tell he was tall and ripped. Wearing dark jeans and boots, it looked like his dark-colored thermal barely contained the muscles of his upper torso. I checked my ogling and was about to pass him when my heel caught in the crack of the floor. I lost my balance and drunkenly fell at the muscular stranger. I thought I would hit the ground, but his arms shot out to catch me.

A spark of electricity immediately made its way down my body as the stranger's strong hands connected with my waist, stunning me into place. I looked up, only to be met with the most enthralling, green eyes I have ever seen. The electric energy caused the air to sizzle, and I could feel the shock all the way down to my fingertips. I knew his body must have had the same reaction as mine when his eyes widened at our contact. As I righted myself, I could only stare at him while I tried to comprehend what happened.

"So-uh, sorry," I stammered. Only the statement was breathless as I forced the words out.

He just stood there with a shocked expression on his face. The peculiar experience was confusing and left both of us trying to catch our breaths. It was only when someone called my name that the spell was broken.

"Henny, are you alright?"

Shit. Gareth. My head turned to the right, and I made eye contact with Gareth as I blinked to clear my head. He looked at me like I had lost my mind. When I turned back around to see the response of the guy, he was nowhere to be found. I stood alone in the hallway.

I turned back to Gareth and made my way to him. I saw that his jaw ticked, indicating that he was not happy that he had to come to the club to retrieve me.

"I see that Jared snitched; that little twerp. I thought for sure he would have lasted longer. Better hope the vampires don't get a hold of him, or he'll share all of our deepest and darkest secrets," I refuted, clearly annoyed at being caught.

Gareth blinked back frustration, sending a pointed look in my direction.

"He was only doing his duty, Henrietta. He did exactly what he should have done and came and got me and Daxon as soon as he got back to the manor."

Ouch, he used my full name. He was pissed. I was annoyed and tipsy. This may not end well.

"Oh, please. He bent easier than a plastic straw and had no problem dropping us off. I should have known he would go running home to you and Dax like the ever-present solider."

"Get real, Henny. You and I both know that it's in no one's best interest to say no to you," he replied.

Did I detect a hint of a smile? I keep eye contact with Gareth, letting him know I was not going to back down.

His eyes softened. "Henny, this is dangerous. After this afternoon, we need to be on full alert and believe me, gin and tonics and Long Islands are not on full alert. You guys cannot think clearly while drinking. I mean, Reed told Daxon how nice his eyebrows looked as soon as she saw him. And she tried to be sexy about it," he said.

At this statement, I literally laughed out loud. If Reed remembered that little bit of information in the morning, she would be absolutely mortified. I'm sure Daxon wouldn't care because he hung on Reed's every word, cheesy or not.

My laugh lessened as Gareth returned my smile. I liked this side of him. He was so much more casual and fun. He must have misunderstood the smile on my face because he took a lock of hair that had fallen out of my braid and brushed it off my shoulder.

"Well, even though I'm not happy that you are here, you look stunning," he said curtly while keeping my gaze.

Yikes, Yikes, Yikes. Was this happening again? I blanched at his statement, cursing that I had sent him the wrong vibe. After that, I worried that someone would see me with Gareth and get the wrong idea. Someone being the stranger who caught me in the hallway. *But wait, why did I even care?*

"Ah, thanks, Gareth," I said as I straightened my dress, breaking eye contact with him. "But we should probably get going before Reed tells Daxon how lovely his arm hair looks."

Disappointed that I did not return his affection, Gareth nodded and turned back around into the throng of people. Before I went back onto the dance floor, I chanced one last look to see if I could, once again, find the most delicious pair of green eyes.

FOUR

COLE

Fuck. Why did I have to touch her? When Bran and I had gone to Fuze, my intention was only to keep an eye on Henrietta and see what she was up to. I knew that Bran would have no issue coming along because it meant he would be able to have a few drinks and talk to some beautiful women, which was his favorite pastime. But after I touched her, things had changed. What the hell had happened when we connected? It felt like a shock had gone through my entire body, and then, it was just us. I was grateful for the reprieve of her friend calling for her. Henny, he called her. *Henny? Even her name was sexy.* At the first opportunity, I bolted, on edge from what happened. I didn't like the feeling; I wasn't one to run.

When we had arrived at the club that evening, I made sure that we were early as I knew that it would be a long wait to get in. Being werewolves, we didn't exactly have the local hook up to this Hunter-owned club. Liam was leery of us going this evening for that exact reason. But I had to go, after seeing her this afternoon, I needed more.

Standing outside, Bran and I were shooting the shit in line when I saw the hunter regulated black Escalade pull up along the curb. *This had to be her.* Once the vehicle slowed to a stop, out walked two beautiful women, who I assumed to be Henny's friends. They were gorgeous; however, they were nothing compared to the goddess that followed.

Henny was wearing a red dress that clung to her body. I thought that she looked good in black earlier, but damn, red was her color. Her pouty red lips begged to be kissed, and I had felt the desire to be the one to do so. Once again, I closed my eyes, taking a deep breath, knowing that this was not the reaction I should be having in her presence. She was a hunter, practically hunter royalty to be exact, and I was a werewolf. Our kinds did not exactly mix. I needed to draw my thoughts to somewhere else. Bran's sudden outburst pulled my attention away from Henny.

"Holy shit, Cole, she is smoking hot. What the fuck, dude, you didn't tell me she was sexy? I get the tall, lanky-ass brother to tail, and you get her? Fuck you, buddy." His carefree comments about her had instantly put me on edge, causing my jaw to tighten. I didn't respond positively to the way he was talking about her or the way he was looking at her as she walked into the club. Chancing one more look at her, I took in the way her legs moved in those fine ass heels—like she owned the place, which wouldn't be surprising if her province did.

"Dude, chill out," I whispered. "Relax, will you? Someone will hear you. She's not a fucking piece of meat so lay off," I spat at Bran, causing him to take a step back from me, his eyebrows raised in question. I sighed at my mistake. I never responded toward women the way I had just reacted toward Henny. He was intrigued by my reaction. *Yeah, well you and me both, buddy.* I heard two girls giggling behind us as Bran had turned in their direction, flashing them one of his signature smiles. Our interaction immediately forgotten.

I rolled my eyes at the attention that Bran was getting, but I was used to it. Women threw themselves at him in the blink of an eye. He was charming, charismatic, and social. I was the exact opposite; quiet, introvert, and a loner. Even being in a pack, I often times enjoyed the pleasure of my own company.

Where our personalities had differed, our physical attributes were similar. Being brothers, Bran and I share a lot of the same features. We were both muscular and tall, standing at six feet, two inches. Liam was not far behind us in height. My whole family shared chestnut brown hair—even Cassie, my nineteen-year-old sister. Each of my siblings was also adorned with brown eyes. My green ones were the exception.

Another round of giggling had brought me back to the present. As charismatic as Bran was, it didn't take much for women to start loitering around him. While he treated women with respect, he still had his fair share of the women around New Orleans. Being werewolves, we mostly kept to ourselves in order to better protect our secret. Unfortunately for the ladies, Bran mostly stuck to casual hookups and cut it off before anything got too serious.

I don't know how he did it. I kept to myself; however, there were a few nights when I welcomed the attention I was receiving to curb the loneliness I felt at not having a mate. I always felt bad when I snuck out the next morning, so I hadn't been with a lot of people. Not to mention there wasn't ever anything *there.*

Even though Bran had always attracted a lot of attention, I still typically brought him out over Liam. Liam would have joined us; however, I felt bad for him coming along while his mate would be left at home. That lucky bastard had found his mate, Lexi, when he had turned eighteen. They have been inseparable ever since.

As we made our way through the line to enter the club, I noticed that the edge to see Henny again returned and was starting to get palpable. Judging by her outfit, I doubted that she was at the club on official business; however, I wouldn't be surprised if something transpired in there. She would be able to take care of herself, though.

Upon finally entering, Bran and I both took in the overwhelming size of this place. It doesn't look this big from the outside.

"I'm going to find a table," I said. "Get us some drinks?"

Bran nodded as he was lost in the sea of people while making his way to the bar. This place was fucking massive, so the girls could be anywhere. With the lights down low and strobes that were blinking rapidly, it was hard to take in the forms all around me.

Once I did a quick sweep of the first floor, I made my way up to the second story where I heard a round of musical laughter. Directly in front of me was Henny and her friends, sitting at a high-top table while a bartender was dropping off a round of drinks. Apparently, the two girls were giving Henny a hard time because she was rolling her eyes as they laughed and continued the conversation. I couldn't take my eyes off of her. In that moment, she seemed so *free*. It had felt like a welcomed breath of fresh air. *Damn, she was so breathtakingly beautiful.* I texted Bran my location and told him to meet me upstairs.

As I waited for Bran to return to the table, Henny must have noticed that eyes were upon her because she was suddenly alert and scanned the area, looking for the source. Not wanting her to notice me, I slipped into the shadows of the archway to become invisible. I had noticed her anxiety, and my eyes were directed to where her hand went on her thigh, which held a thigh holster and an attached dagger. *This girl was going to kill me.* As if she could get any sexier.

Letting the tension relax in her shoulders, Henny relented her search and directed her focus back to her friends after they noticed what was happening. Bran made his way next to me while winking at the few girls next to us.

"Did I miss anything?" he asked as I grabbed the Jameson from his hands and threw it back. His eyes had gone back and forth between Henny and me as my gaze had locked onto her. "Uh huh, I'm sure I didn't," he said with a chuckle, but I wasn't paying attention to him, I was paying attention to her.

As the evening went by, it was obvious that I was not the only man whose attention was on the table of women in front of me. Guys were coming up to them left and right, but it always seemed like Henny had sent them packing. Was she sending them away because she was seeing someone? I didn't see a significant other or mate listed in the notes Liam had sent me. *Thank God.*

Rounds of drinks came and went, and I had suddenly gone on alert when I noticed that Henny was standing, announcing to the world that she was going to dance. Moving from the table, she stumbled a little as she pulled her friends down to the first-floor dance floor. Not caring that Bran was calling after me, I found myself striding over to the railing to watch as the three of them had begun to dance without a care in the world. The way she was moving her body was even more intoxicating than the drink I was sipping on. I took a long swig of my drink, trying to settle the urge inside of me to meet her downstairs. *Remember what you're here for.*

But it felt as if everyone else had disappeared around her, making her the only woman in the room. The sensual way she was moving those perfect, beautiful hips made me want to run my fingers along her body while she arched into me the way she was arching her neck on the dance floor. Watching her move combined with the light layer of sweat that was covering every inch of her body, I was losing it.

When she looked like she was telling her friends she was going to the bathroom, I did exactly what I shouldn't have done. I had followed her, needing to keep my eyes on her. I waited until she was a considerable distance away when I walked past Bran, who had a woman on each side of him eating out of the palm of his hand. Normally, this annoyed me; however, I didn't care what he was doing.

"I'm going to the bathroom," I said not making eye contact with him as I passed by and not even knowing if he had responded. I wanted to catch up with her fast because I didn't want to lose her in the throng of people.

Making my way to the back of the dance floor, the ambient lighting of the area Henny had just walked through cast the passageway in a dark, erotic glow. The second she stepped out of the bathroom, I felt her presence everywhere. I wasn't even sure how this was happening since this was the closest I'd ever been to her. Her sexy figure was making her way toward me, and the closer she got, the more impatient I became. I was just going to let her pass when all of a sudden, she lost her balance. Out of instinct, my arms shot out to catch her.

When I touched her silky, smooth, skin, it felt like my body was on fire. She obviously had the same reaction because her eyes were as wide as saucers. *Were her eyes pink?* But it must have been a trick of the lighting because they went back to the most severe shade of blue. The heat on my skin was increasing the longer that I held onto her, and all I could do was stare at her. She was overwhelming.

"So-uh, sorry," she stammered out noticing my reaction to her.

At the end of the hallway, someone called her name and asked if she was all right. Immediately looking to the source of the intrusion, I dropped my hands off of her body and took off. I was irritated that another man was holding her attention, but I needed to get out of there and gather my thoughts.

I rounded the corner to the point where I was no longer visible, but I could still see what she was doing. She walked to the man that had called her name and started a conversation with him, clearly still on edge from our interaction. I didn't like how casual their conversation was. It looked like she put him at ease. I was longing for her to talk to me like that.

Then, that asshole reached out his hand and brushed a piece of hair off her shoulder, and his fingers lingered on her collarbone. I felt rage seep into my body at the thought of his touch. *You don't even know her, calm down,* I had to remind myself, taking deep, calming breaths to ease my nerves. If I kept this up, I would be in jeopardy of shifting.

One thing that did calm me down was the way she reacted to his touch. She flinched back as if the intimate gesture was not welcomed. The second I got back to our cabin, I was going to see who this guy was and if she had any relationship with him. I prayed to God that she didn't.

They must have ended their conversation because the blond-haired man turned to walk back toward the dance floor. With one last look

B. K. Rae

in the direction of our encounter, Henny turned her eyes to where we once stood. After a small sigh, Henny turned and followed him.

The second she left, I had felt a little bit of pressure lift off my body. I have no idea why I had that type of reaction to her, or why I felt drawn to her. But there was one thing I knew, in regards to Henny Bradford, I was in trouble.

FIVE

HENNY

I lay in bed longer than I should the next morning, contemplating my current state of mind. The raid followed by Reed's birthday was more exhaustive than it should have been. Coming home last night, I still got flashes of the warm sensation caressing my skin, and I felt remnants of the electric shock from the stranger who caught me. Every time I closed my eyes after lying down, a pair of electric green irises stared back at me. What was that reaction that we had to each other's touch? I have never experienced anything like that before, and it unnerved me a little more than it should. I don't get unsettled easily. I finally fell into a fitful sleep, hoping I felt better the next day.

Trying to pull myself out of bed, Reed dragged herself into my room. Her messy red curls were thrown into a bun on the top of her head, and she looked about as bad as I felt.

"I'm never drinking again," she said as she pulled back my blankets and climbed into bed with me. So much for being productive. I smiled at the awkward things she said to my brother.

"Actually, I thought you were a blast to be around last night. The things that came out of your mouth were the best I've heard yet. I think I'm actually going to use them as pick-up lines one day," I said, laughing at the memory.

Reed threw her head into her hands and shook it, burrowing further into the mess of sheets and pillows.

"Stop beating yourself up, you weren't even that bad. Believe me, I've acted way worse. Don't even act like Daxon will think any less of you because you were drunk rambling last night," I responded to her, trying to ease her embarrassment. Reed peeked at me through the fingers she spread across her face.

"Dax and I kissed last night," she said as she turned fifty shades of pink.

I gaped. "What the hell!" I said as I took a pillow out from under her and smacked her with it. "Maybe you should lead with that next time! I can't believe you didn't tell me right away!" She looked at me as she couldn't believe that I acted that way.

"Hen, I was scared to tell you," she said suddenly serious.

I laughed and kissed her on her cheek. "Reed, there are two people in this world that I know better than myself, and that's you and my brother. Trust me, I've known you guys have liked each other since you knocked him down in training when we were five."

"You're not mad?" she asked one more time as a sincere look crossed her face.

"Of course not, I'm just finally glad it's out in the open. The awkward sexual tension between you two chokes me half the time."

This time she was the one to smack me with the pillow while I laughed. She went on to reiterate the events that led to the kiss.

"We were being a little flirty, and then he got out of the car to help me down. I slipped off the step. His arms wrapped around me, catching me. I looked up to see his face, and I couldn't help it. Before I knew it, I reached up to kiss him. I was worried he would pull away at first because he froze, but then he kissed me back," she said as she sighed, replaying the memory in her head with passion in her eyes.

I was thoughtful, she had an interaction last night where strong arms wrapped around her causing her to go still? That makes two of us. Green eyes floated back to my memory.

"If kissing him felt that good after drinking, then I can't imagine what kissing him would be like. . .not drinking. I mean if he wants to kiss me again," she said suddenly, a little worried.

I rolled my eyes at the sentiment. "My Brother has been waiting to kiss you for years. Trust me, he will want to kiss you again."

She relaxed at my statement and smiled at me. She grabbed the clicker to the television in my room and turned it on as we both refused to get out of bed. As she lay there in a state of pure bliss watching some reality tv show, I dozed off as my mind went back to the stranger I couldn't get out of my head.

Sometime mid-afternoon, Nessa came and dragged Reed and me out of bed. Even though we were off, I changed to get a little bit of training in. Hopefully, it would calm some of this nervous energy. As I made my way to the training room, I saw Daxon coming toward me in the hall, and he instantly broke into a smile. I couldn't help it, I smiled at his reaction, it was infectious. Once I reached my twin, I gave him a high five which he proudly returned needing no explanation what it was for.

"Good job, it's about damn time," I exclaimed.

"Thank you," he answered as he was looking down at his shoes and. . .blushing? My brother did not blush.

"Although, Reed is worried that you are only interested in drunk Reed, so you better keep the smooches coming," I winked.

"Oh, they're going to keep coming," he replied as his smile became more pronounced. But then he turned somber.

"I'm glad you're here, I came to get you. Dad and Gareth are in the office. Something happened last night that we need to talk about," he answered in a regretful tone.

I instantly transitioned into hunter mode. Dad made it a point that we were off the next two days, so whatever happened was damaging.

Even though we broke up a huge vampire ring with the raid yesterday, we knew that the vampires were looking for something and I felt this had something to do with it. I turned around and walked with Daxon to the office where our dad was. My dad and Gareth didn't even acknowledge our presence, as they were leaning over a set of pictures.

"Hello darling," my dad said in a mournful tone as he looked up from the photos.

He must have been up all night because he looked exhausted. I suddenly felt guilty for going out last night. For my dad not to say anything about it meant that it was the least of his worries right now. I walked over to my dad and Gareth to find out what happened.

"What's going on?" I asked.

Gareth met my gaze with a dismal look in his eyes.

"We found another group of girls last night," my dad stated, and that's all I needed to hear.

Continuing to look at him, I understood what that meant. We thought that we took down a major nest; however, this meant that it was not the main one in New Orleans—like we were looking for.

"Shit," I whispered, grinding my teeth together. "Where?"

"Just outside the bayou," my dad responded as he slid the pictures my way.

Weird. "But that's not their normal territory?" I questioned, trying to make sense of this.

"That's what we thought. It's possible they are on to us and knew where we're actively raiding," he said.

I thought about it for a second. *But that means. . .* "You think someone from the inside is feeding them information?" I asked, shocked at the accusation.

We all remained quiet for a few moments, taking that in before Gareth broke the silence. "We think that they are sending a message, a message showing that we can't stop them."

Anger coiled within me. "The hell we can't!" I responded as I tossed the pictures onto my father's desk. Gareth was right, they were trying to send the message that they were untouchable. The vampires were getting bold as of late, and it made me nervous that something was changing. Something was coming.

"Are we sure about that?" Daxon questioned, and we all stared at him with confusion, so he continued. "Sending a message, that could be any type of supernatural. Female, male, young or old, but these girls—they are young. These girls are human. All between nineteen to twenty-five years old? This isn't about power, they are looking for something, looking for someone."

My father and I looked at each other, digesting the severity of Daxon's statement. I rolled my head, trying to free some of the tension of the conversation. Gareth spoke next.

"Henny, we think they are trying to draw female hunters out by making them feel obligated to rescue the human girls. We've been talking, and we think. . ." he said as he looked at my father, who nodded for him to go on. "We think that it's best if you lay low for a while, Nessa and Reed, too. After what happened, last night could have been—"

"I'm going to stop you right there," I said as I held up my hands. "We're highly-trained hunters that went out to relieve some stress for a birthday. You know those days where we celebrate our birth each year that we remain alive because of what we do every day? We're twenty-two, not twelve. It's not like I walked into a vampire nest with some girlfriends looking for trouble. Also, I'm not going to hide inside because someone or something *might* be looking for someone who resembles a variety of women my age. I'm not that kind of girl, and you know it," I fired back as the tension became thick in the room. I was irritated with the way Gareth responded, and we were now locked in a stare-down when my father chimed in.

"Henny, I would have to agree. Until things cool down, you need to lay low. I don't need you going in half-cocked like you did yesterday."

"But—" I started, but he stopped me.

"That's an order," my father responded. For the first time in my life, he ordered not to do something.

I felt shock at the statement as I stood there, mouth open wide. For one, I was upset that my father sided with Gareth, but secondly, I had an inkling of what was happening. If what I thought were correct, my father had just cause for his statement. I nodded, respecting his orders but still harboring resentment at the command.

"Why don't you get some training in," he said. "We have to figure out hunting parties and see if we can get one more raid in tonight."

Annoyed that I wasn't involved, I stalked out of the room and went right to the training center. I was so angry and upset about what happened. While I was out partying and enjoying the night, those young girls were sucked dry. Rage rolled through my body.

Barging into the training center, I went right to a punching bag to release some of my aggression. I heard the door open behind me, but I didn't take notice. I was too interested in what was in front of me. As I jabbed right hooks and uppercuts into the bag, my father rounded the corner and came into view. I stopped punching long enough to readjust the tape on my hands. I looked up at him, taking notice of the distressed features of his face. Standing there, he put his hands in his pockets when he spoke.

"When I was your age, I had been called to, what seemed like, a routine assignment. Go in, get eyes on the target, make sure the target was safe, and then get out. Be the guardian. Give a status report and then leave. It was that simple. I looked at the address and seen that it was a bar, so I didn't mind. I would go in, have a beer and just wait and see what happened," my father looked reminiscent. "I heard that door chime and in walked your mother. As she lowered her hood, it was as if the world stopped turning. God, she was the most beautiful thing I had ever seen, until you were born," he gave a small smile. He was thoughtful, and it made me beam. "Her presence was commanding. She didn't have a fear in the world. I had almost forgotten what I was doing there, and as if she heard my thoughts, her eyes connected with mine, and she smiled. I was your mother's ever since. In the weeks that followed meeting her, I couldn't stay away from her and learned as much about her as I could. She was passionate, determined, and she fought so hard for what she believed in. She didn't take shit from anyone."

I relished in the information he shared. I could tell my mother's death was still hard for my father as he rarely talked about her in this capacity. This is the most open he's been about it. Hearing him speak about her like this was entrancing.

"One of your mother's best qualities was that she cared so deeply for what she believed in and the people she loved. So very much like you. The burdens that she carried were too strong for any one person, and I was happy that I was there to help her through a lot of it. Had I not been, I'm afraid it would have broken her."

My eyes stung because he had just described how I had felt on a daily basis. Some days, the pressure overwhelmed me.

My father walked over to me, taking my face in his hands. "You are so much like her that some days when you walk into the room, I have to check to make sure it's not her. But Henny, I'm sorry. I'm not willing to make a sacrifice that would jeopardize your safety. Something is happening, and until we figure out what it is, I need you to be okay with this. I can't lose you, too," he finished as he brought me into a fierce hug. "I worry that because your mother wasn't around, I made you and Dax grow up too fast. We'll get this figured out, but in the meantime, please, stay out of trouble," he said as he pulled back and eyed me expectantly. "Relax, go shopping or something," he laughed.

I pulled away with my nose scrunched because that did not sound appealing. I liked to dress up and go out, but shopping, meh. It took hours I didn't have.

"Maybe even go on a date?" my father cocked an eyebrow.

"Bleh," I said with a sour taste in my mouth as I give him a playful push back, and my father smiled at the reaction.

"I would feel so much better if you were able to find someone. I worry about you. I want to know that you are taken care of. I won't always be around," he looked at me expectantly.

Standing straighter, I put my hands on my hips. "Believe me, I am very capable of taking care of myself, thank you very much."

"Oh, I know you are," he laughed, but then suddenly grew serious. "I want you to have someone you can rely on and share some of the burdens you carry, like I had with your mother. You know Gareth—"

"Oh God, Dad, please—don't," I responded. We've had this conversation before. Gareth was a close friend to me but nothing more. He was just as much as a brother to me as Daxon. Although he has been a little touchy lately, I'd have to address that.

"Alright, Alright, I just thought I'd give it one more chance," he said palms up, surrendering. "Please take it easy tonight, I mean it, Henny," my dad gave me another hug and then left the room.

I contemplated our discussion as I stood there taking a deep breath, trying to calm the vast array of emotions I felt. Guilt for what happened last night, anger for being restricted in my actions, and for the first time, loneliness. For the first time in my life, I felt like an outcast.

Regaining my bearings, I worked out for another hour. My mind reeled at my father's words. Heading back to my room, calmness filled the hallways of the manor as the evening was quiet. I stopped short of my father's office, just outside the cracked door. I looked in at my dad, Gareth, and a few other hunters huddled over a floor plan, putting together a few more teams to go on one more raid this evening. Daxon and I made eye contact, an apology in his gaze. I turned around, filled with disappointment. I should be with them. It was eerily quiet as I walked back to my room. I hadn't seen any other hunters, but that didn't mean they weren't around. After taking a shower, I lay down closing my eyes, only to fall into a deep sleep.

When I awoke, darkness seeped in through my bedroom window, and I cursed to myself for sleeping so long. I walked back to the bathroom to splash cold water on my face, trying to erase the fogginess I felt.

Making my way down the hall to Reed's bedroom, I knocked, only to be met with silence.

"Reed?" I said as I opened the door, only her room was empty. *Weird.* We were explicitly told to stay put tonight.

I went to Nessa and Tate's quarters, and it was empty as well. *Had everyone already gone out on the raid? Maybe I slept longer than I thought?* As I made my way back to my room, I heard the ping of a text message. I walked over to my bedside table to grab my phone. I had to look twice to check the message that flashed across my screen.

SOS, NEED YOU NOW!

My heart skipped a beat. I dialed Reed to see what was going on only to be sent directly to voicemail. Another text chimed in.

Can't talk, they will hear. Please come. Warehouse at Main St and Carpenter.

My response was instant.

What happened, are you okay?

I was met with silence. I tore out of my room, searching the common areas for someone, only the manor was vacant. I then remembered that everyone was most likely on the raid, so that meant Reed could really be in trouble. I tried calling my father and Daxon, but it just kept ringing. Gareth's call went right to voicemail.

Anxiety flowed through me as I ran to the security office, grabbing the first pair of keys I could find, which just happened to be a V-8 Mustang. *Perfect.* Racing out to the garage, I pressed the key fob to locate the car and hopped in. I started the ignition and backed up into the night, speeding away to save my best friend.

SIX

COLE

I had finally felt like I was recovering from the effects of the previous night. After I had my run-in with Henny, I had been on edge, as if the shock I had received had changed my body chemistry. One thing for certain was that I couldn't get her off my mind. The previous night was on a constant loop in my head.

After our connection, I took off, mostly out of surprise. Turning the corner of the hallway, finally out of her line of vision, I rested my hands on my knees and took a deep breath trying to relax the electrical vibe that was flowing through me. I had waited in the shadows until she was out of sight, then took off toward the balcony to Bran, whose confusion sprouted on his face.

"We're going," I gritted out, passing right by him.

"What the hell?" he questioned as he started to stand, sending a silent apology to the women he was speaking with. He may not have wanted to leave, but he followed me out of there without an argument.

We walked to the car in silence. Anxious, I was practically racing to the car, but Bran's pace kept up with mine. Once we were in the vehicle, he turned to me, questioning what happened.

"You going to tell me why the hell you went tearing out of there?" he asked. "Or why you no longer care about what Henrietta Bradford is doing?"

The mere mention of Henny made me tense as I gripped the steering wheel and peeled out of the parking lot. I was trying not to let him notice the effect she had on me, but I was failing miserably.

"Alright, whatever, bro," he said as he threw up his hands. We both remained silent the remainder of the ride.

Once we got back to our cabin, I went straight to the second story, knocking on Liam's door even at the late hour. I needed answers, and I needed them now. When supernatural beings have connections like that, it typically means only one thing. And that one thing could not happen.

"So, Henrietta Bradford," Bran asked again casually leaning against the wall with his arms crossed over his chest as we were waiting for Liam to answer the door.

"Don't even fuckin' talk about her," I snarled, annoyed by his interruption. He looked at me with an eyebrow raised. *Shit.* Pinching the bridge of my nose, I closed my eyes and sighed in defeat. He baited me, and I played right into his hands. Now he knows something happened, and Henny was behind it. Flashes of the memory had kept floating before my eyes. The color of her eyes, the shape of her hips, and damn, that fucking dress. She was perfection. Growing impatient, I knocked on the door again.

As the door flung open, Lexi's small frame stood in the doorway. She gave me a small smile and held the door back signaling for us to enter the room. She kissed both Bran and me on the cheek as we walked in before she made her way back to the living area of their suite. When I rounded the corner, Liam was standing there with a concerned look on his face. I was surprised they were still up, but I suspected it was because Liam was waiting for us to get back.

"Lexi, can we have a second with Liam?" It meant to come out polite, but it sounded impatient, forced. Giving me a questioning gaze, she looked at Liam and then shook her head.

"I'll let you guys have the room," she said as she walked over to Liam, giving him a kiss, then going to the bedroom. It wasn't until I heard the door click that both Liam and Bran's attention was on me. I walked over to the windowpane, placing both of my palms on the edge. I rolled my neck while figuring out how to word what I was going to ask next. I could feel the gaze of both of them searing into the back of my head, waiting for me to speak. Bran was fidgeting, and Liam looked concerned. Turning to face them, I rapped my knuckle on the wood while biting my lip trying to manage the stress I was feeling when it just came out.

"What happens during a mate connection?" I asked, and upon my question, both of my brothers froze, their breathing halted. *They weren't expecting that.* I also heard a short intake of breath from the bedroom. In all honestly, Lexi could have just stayed out here, with our supernatural hearing, it didn't matter where she was, she would have heard the conversation.

"No. You fucking didn't?" Bran questioned with a look of mock horror on his face.

"Bran," Liam warned as he held his hand out to the side, thwarting Bran from making additional comments never taking his eyes away from mine. Taking a deep breath, he continued.

"It's undeniable. When you meet your mate for the first time, the world closes in around you and time stops. Once you are in their presence, it's like no else ever existed, and in that moment, you learn that your reason for being is solely for them. No other will ever compare."

"And when you touch?" I questioned.

Liam looked thoughtful and sympathetic as he understood what was happening. "It's like nothing you've ever felt. It's shocking, figuratively and literally. When you touch them, there is no mistaking, you know."

I nodded slowly as I contemplated his words, coming to the realization of what I had expected on the drive home.

Liam took a few slow steps toward me as he reflected on my questions. He knew what I was doing tonight and the reason that I was out.

"You had a mate connection tonight, didn't you?" he asked.

I looked him square in the eyes. "Yes," I replied hoarsely.

"It was with her?" he asked, and all I could do was nod a second time.

"Oh, shit," Bran spoke glancing between the two of us.

I should have never gotten that close, and I definitely shouldn't have touched her. It appeared that fate had different plans. Maybe if Bran had trailed her like he wanted to, this could have all been avoided. However, mates were typically fated, so if she were truly destined to be mine, destiny would have found a way. The reality of the situation had just been confirmed. If what he described was true, I, an Alpha werewolf, just had a mate connection with Henny Bradford, potentially the next in line to rule the hunter race.

After my conversation with Bran and Liam, any attempt to sleep or function that evening was out of the question. The information that we had discussed was overwhelming, and I could feel my chest tighten. Upon waking the next morning, I felt as if I were in a fog, only half listening and responding to everything that was happening around me. As if on auto pilot, I found myself behind the wheel of my truck, pulling out of the cabin. I drove around for hours trying to sort everything out. I didn't even realize that I had pulled into the rear parking lot of Bradford Manor until I was putting the vehicle into park. *What are you doing here?* I thought. Even in my confused daze, my body subconsciously brought me to her. Thankfully, it was easier to remain hidden now that it was well into the evening.

I took a deep breath. Sitting outside of the Bradford Manor, keeping watch. I used the silence to try and sort everything out. I had to be as close to her as possible, it was like my body was unconsciously being called to her presence. Being the loner of the bunch, I wasn't actively looking for the company of a mate, and here she came slamming me with a force I couldn't deny.

After my brothers and I had discussed what happened, Liam received a phone call from a neighboring pack in Atlanta. Their Alpha, Landon, confirmed that another vampire attack had occurred. The hunters would definitely be on guard, if not planning another strike after this. That was two major attacks in just as many days. From my previous knowledge, hunter mentality would be to strike hard and strike fast. They would likely retaliate tonight.

I was lost in my train of thought when a black mustang came tearing out of the manor, and I caught a small glimpse of who it was. Henny.

"Shit," I murmured to myself as I fumbled with my keys, trying to start my vehicle. Once I righted myself, I started the truck and sped to follow after her. Judging by the urgency she left the premises, something was wrong.

I had almost lost her a few times as I was barreling behind a few car lengths back, trying to remain hidden. She glided in and out of traffic with ease, and it wasn't until she turned left down the main road that I noticed she was going down to the old warehouse district. In that area, there was nothing but abandoned buildings for days. *What the hell was she doing?* Maybe she was going to meet with someone or she had backup in the car? Either way, I continued to follow. Fresh tire tracks were leading up to the warehouse where she had stopped. Once I turned onto the drive, I came upon the black mustang with the driver's door open, lights still turned on, and keys in the ignition. Henny was nowhere in sight. Something was definitely wrong; my wolf was now sensing it. *Follow her.*

Scrambling out of the truck, I surveyed the area using my heightened senses to grasp what the fuck was going on. I closed my eyes, calling the wolf forward. I was able to pinpoint her breathing and heartbeat. Her heartrate was erratic and her emotions were. . . frightened? *Danger.* I needed to get to her, and I needed to get to her fast.

I ran to the entrance of the warehouse and was met with silence. I detected further movement, and my blood ran cold when I took in that the motions were not accompanied by active heartrates. *Vampires.* As

I entered the warehouse, my mind was racing and panic set in at the thought of finding her in time. Distant echoing and labored breathing informed me that she was being chased, and at that moment, all that mattered was getting to Henny. Racing, I followed the sound of the footsteps and then finally caught an image of the vampires that were chasing her.

"She's heading toward the door!" a vampire shouted. I could feel my eyes start to change and I knew a vivid glow would be emanating from them, my vision became even more refined. I had no control of what happened next.

Feeling the cracking that I had grown accustomed to, it only took moments before I shifted. After his statement, rage consumed me at the thought of something harming Henny and my Alpha took over. Now in wolf form, I sent a message to Liam and Bran, hoping they would receive it. I took off as I made my way deeper into the warehouse. With a newfound velocity, I crossed the viaducts and cut off one of the vampires as he was stalking his way toward her. Wolf instinct took over, and as I reached him, I leaped onto his body extending his neck. It only took a few seconds for me to get him into position, and with a snap, the vampire fell limply to the floor. Looking up, I made eye contact with a second vampire as Henny turned to defend herself. *What the fuck was she doing?* And that's when she noticed me behind the remaining vampire, her eyes wide as she stood rooted in position.

Pushing harder for the second vampire, I made it to him in seconds. Henny was slowly backing away as she never took her eyes off the situation. After a few steps, she turned and was hurtling toward the door.

The second vampire had been stronger and a better fighter, and as I was trying to end him, I noticed that Henny's exit was blocked by a tall guy. *Is that the guy that stopped her last night?*

Trying to remain in the moment, it was hard not to pick up on the different emotions that were flowing through her system. Pain, confusion, disgust. It dawned on me, he wasn't here to help her, he was

49

here to take her. One of her own. Her feelings were feeding into me, increasing my rage tenfold.

"You son of a bitch!" I heard her scream, and I fought harder to reach her.

His smile was menacing. "Sorry, darling," he replied.

I finally overcame the vampire in front of me and snapped the creature's neck. Henny hesitated for a second, looking in my direction, and that's when the hunter lashed out at her, striking her forehead. All I saw was red.

It wasn't until the last second that he saw me coming, and the look on my face must have been murderous because his fear reflected back at me. While fighting him, I saw out of the corner of my eye that Henny was losing consciousness. The man used my moment of hesitation as an opportunity to make his escape. Had Henny not been bleeding profusely, I would have followed him and ended his existence. Henny yelled from her knees trying to keep herself upright.

"Yeah, you better fucking run!" she yelled.

I laughed, using the calming emotion to shift back. Even as she was about to lose consciousness, vanity shined through, and my heart expanded at her comment because if she were gravely injured, she wouldn't have needed to mock that he was running. I couldn't help but chuckle at her proclamation as I made my way to her, realizing I had shifted so fast that I didn't have clothes to get back into. This could get awkward. But she didn't seem to notice as her face was glued to mine. Even in her state, recognition dawned in her eyes.

"You," she barely made out as she recognized me.

Whatever I felt at the club last night, she must have felt it, too. "It's okay, I'm not going to hurt you," I said as gently as I could. Holding my palms up in surrender, I didn't want to frighten her, knowing my eyes still held the glow from shifting. Her injury was taking over as she tried to stand but slipped to her knees. I sprang forward to catch her as she lost consciousness in my arms. Scooping her up, I pulled her close just to relish in the relief of her being safe. I ran my nose along her neck checking for a pulse. The slow rhythm of her beating heart assured me. Once I confirmed she was okay, I needed to get her looked at and took her to the one place she belonged at that moment, home.

SEVEN

HENNY
Present Day

I awoke to the soft sounds of traffic filtering in through the open window, and a dog was barking in the distance. A single car horn sounded. The cool breeze that coasted in comforted and soothed me. I tried to wake up, but the fogginess lingered. I rolled over and took in the dark blue pillow on the bed, inhaling the rich, deep scent. These pillows smelled amazing. Taking in one more deep breath, awareness worked its way into my mind, and I froze. This was not my bedroom. Now on full alert, I opened both of my eyes and was hit with a sudden wave of nausea and pain in my temples. My heart rate increased as I continued to search my surroundings. The events of last night flooded back into me. Images flashed in my memory: the text messages, the warehouse, Gareth, the wolf, and green eyes. *Those green eyes.* I slowly sat up, taking in the room before me.

The setup was sleek and open. The walls were brick with floor length windows on the right side of me facing the street. Through those windows was a balcony, giving the most perfect view of the city. Dark wood floors filtered through the apartment and black iron pillars were strategically placed from floor to ceiling through the area. The place was clean but masculine. Dark colors adorned all the rustic furniture that encompassed what looked like a small studio apartment. Straightening even further, the bathroom and kitchen came into view, as well as the front door to the apartment. I ran my fingers over the softness of the king-size bed I currently occupied. Lost in the fabric, I didn't hear him approach.

"How are you feeling?" he said softly.

I snapped my head to the voice that just spoke. I inhaled a deep breath as my body recognized the energy that buzzed through my system. He looked so familiar, I squinted as if that would make my memory return. The night of Reed's birthday visited my mind, and I realized that the guy from the club stood before me. He took a few steps closer to me.

He was as tall and built like I remembered. A dark blue t-shirt clung to his chest and shoulders like it was made to fit his body. Jeans that fit him in all the right places hung low on his hips. His eyes stood out against his dark brown hair, and his bronzed skin looked like he spent endless hours in the sun. Facial hair covered enough that it was attractive, but not overbearing. The sexiest freckle sat on the right side of his face, just below his cheekbone.

Recognizing my awkward gawking, his face broke into a breathtaking smirk as he cleared his throat again. The action brought me back to reality so quickly that I was able to shake the haziness residing in my brain and spoke.

"I'm sorry, what?" My response came out more breathless than I intended it to, but his good looks caught me off guard.

"I was wondering how you were feeling," he repeated, still smirking. Cleary, he had picked up on the effect he had on me as I gazed gracelessly at him long enough for him to change the subject.

"Do you remember anything that happened last night?"

This brought me back, and I nodded solemnly. "Thank you," I managed to get out before he asked further information.

When I responded to Reed's texts, the information led me to an empty warehouse. Had the stranger before me just been around that area and heard the commotion? Had he seen the vampires? As hunters, we have the same physical features of humans but our excessive speed, strength, and agility is anything but. If he had seen Gareth only, I could play this as a physical assault gone wrong, but if he had seen anything with the vampires, that would be a lot harder to explain.

"How did you find me?" I asked as he came even closer, never taking his eyes off mine, which caused my skin to flush. My body now fought the urge to bolt to the door because of how nervous he made me. Not the type of nervous that I felt when in danger, but the type of nervous that has sin written all over it.

"I was in the area when I heard a struggle. Once I entered the building, I found you getting clocked on the side of the head."

Maybe he saw more than I thought? I nodded slowly and was suddenly hit with the need to move. Pushing back the covers, I swung my legs over the side of the bed. The swift movement caused pain to radiate behind my eyes, and I stumbled forward. He rushed around and grabbed my arms to steady me. Once again, the energy circulated through my body from the tip of my hair down to my toes. As if he had felt the same connection, he quickly released my arms.

A little perturbed by his reaction to me, I shot a question his way. "Do you make it a habit to lurk around empty warehouses to provide aid when needed?" I asked as I tried to ignore the energy buzzing between us.

Amused by my response, his eyebrows inched up. "Do you normally make it a habit to run into a warehouse full of vampires when you're by yourself, waiting for men like me to provide aid when needed?"

Yikes. "Vampires? Really?" I chuckled awkwardly. "And I thought I was the one who hit my head." I looked back into those alluring green eyes only to find annoyance staring back at me.

"You and I both know there were vampires in the warehouse last night. I was painfully aware of them as I eliminated them from the

A Hunter's Fate

situation. You were scared enough that I heard your heart pounding in your chest as you were running away from them and trying to find an escape route. I'm not sure what you're doing right now, but you're not fooling anyone."

I glared at him as he finished his berating. "I appreciate that you helped me, really, I do. But I'm not sure what you think you saw last night, but trust me, it wasn't vampires," I replied, standing taller, ignoring the screaming pain in my temples. He met my stance, and I noticed that he was at least a foot taller, if not more, than my tiny frame. He took another step toward me and my traitorous heartrate spiked.

I met his gaze, showing him that I wasn't afraid as we remained locked in a stare-down. We were only inches apart, and our chests almost touched. He wasn't backing down? I wasn't either. "So, you heard my heartbeat and just had to come to my rescue from vampires? Does that mean you are some kind of superhero with supernatural hearing?" I asked, mocking him.

"No," he replied flatly. "But being a werewolf helps."

55

EIGHT

COLE

I instantly regretted the response as soon as it came out of my mouth. If Henny wasn't alert before, she was now. The color drained from her face as she processed my words. Her eyes shot to the door, and as soon as I realized what she was planning, I tried to embrace her arm to show her she was okay. Big mistake.

With a speed I had definitely not anticipated given her injury, she grabbed my arm just before it touched her skin. She pulled me forward using her other arm to elbow me in the face. As action thrust me downward, she used her legs to take out my knees, and as they hit the floor, she jumped over me. Sprinting toward the door, she'd be free in seconds.

What she didn't expect was that my speed was equal to hers. I leaped up, shooting forward while wrapping my arms around her waist while she tried to lash out again.

"Stop, stop!" I repeated. "I'm not going to hurt you," I shouted, trying to gain control of her as she spun around to take another swing. She was flinching in pain, and it was then that I noticed the injury on her head had broken open, probably from the force she was exhibiting. She was getting sloppy in her movements as she tried to fight the ache. Tangling in one another, I finally grabbed ahold of both of her wrists and had spun her around, so her back was to me. A slight sigh escaped from her lips.

"Please, listen to me. I'm not going to hurt you," I whispered in her ear. "If I was going to hurt you, don't you think I would have had the opportunity already?"

She stood silently to contemplate the words, I became aware of the close contact I had with her body. I took in the goosebumps that my whisper had caused. Her breathing had become erratic.

"I'm going to let go of you, alright? I'm not going to hurt you, but I need you to move slowly because it looks like you reopened the wound from last night. I need to take a look at it, okay?"

I slowly released her, sidestepping toward the door so she wouldn't try to bolt again. As she turned around, her eyes connected with mine, and she was contemplating trusting me.

"Okay, werewolf, start explaining," she said as she narrowed her eyes at me, awaiting an answer.

I tried to hide the smile that broke through at her defiance, which earned me a glare from those beautiful, blue eyes. "Okay, I'll tell you what you want to know, but I need to look at your head first. The bathroom is behind you to the right. I have the medical supplies in there." I motioned my arm for her to turn toward the bathroom.

Rocking back and forth on her heels biting her lip, she turned around and headed in the direction of the bathroom. Henny walked into the bathroom and sat on the toilet. She sat with both her arms and legs crossed as she was waiting for me to start explaining. I started digging through the medical supplies that Lexi had left last night.

On the way back to the apartment, I called Liam to explain what happened and they jumped in the car, no questions asked. Liam and Lexi had sprung into action when I had walked into my apartment with an unconscious Henny in my arms. As I placed her in my bed,

Lexi treated the wound while I explained to Liam what had happened. I never left her side.

I had what I needed after rummaging through the medicine cabinet. I kneeled down in front of Henny so that we were eye level, dabbing some alcohol onto a cotton pad. "I'm Cole Martin," I said as I brushed a piece of her hair back to gain access to her injury. I could feel her eyes boring into my face. She waited a few seconds to respond.

"I'm Henny Bradford."

"I know," I replied. As soon as my response exited my mouth, she glared at me for what I'm sure she felt was an invasion of privacy. I held up the clean bandages showing her that I was going to change her dressings.

"Continue," she ground out.

"I'm part of a small pack that resides here in New Orleans. We keep to ourselves, but we picked up on more frequent vampire attacks. It was well hidden to the public, but we noticed. We were surprised there hadn't been an intervention from the hunters as we have been hearing rumors that you were instituting harsher punishments," I said, and I felt her stiffen. I paused, bringing the gauze to her head, and she winced at the contact. "We knew something was up as it's not Jonah's style to turn a blind eye. As a result, we started tracking the movements of your family to see what was changing. Judging by the events that occurred last night, we have a much more serious issue on our hands."

"We?" Henny asked as I continued to put fresh gauze on her wound.

"Me and my family. We're all werewolves. I have two brothers and a sister and my brother's mate." She stared at me as she was waiting for me to elaborate further. "We divided up the different hunters in your family to track and follow your movements to see if we could find anything out. As you may have already gathered, I was assigned to you, which is why I knew you were in the warehouse last night. I knew you needed help."

"How long have you been following me?" Henny inquired.

"Not very long, a few days. I was around but never got close, until the other night."

Henny sucked in her breath as her eyes widened realization crossing her face. I knew exactly what she was thinking. "That was you in the club wasn't it? In the hallway?" she asked.

I nodded. "That was me."

The energy buzzing between us was manageable before, but now, it was palpable.

"And the werewolf at the warehouse?" she inquired.

"Also me," I responded as I set the medical supplies down next to me, now resting my forearms on my knees.

"You saved my life," she replied looking away, shaking her head. "After the warehouse is a little fuzzy," she said as she made eye contact with me once more. "Obviously, I made it back here. Did you treat me? These clothes are not the clothes that I had on last night."

My face flooded with heat at the insinuation of her words. That I changed and unclothed that beautiful body. *I wish.* Needing a moment to think, I stood as I started putting the supplies away. "I was worried that your head wound was severe so I called in my brother and his mate. She's what you could call a healer. She tended to you privately, so no, I did not witness you getting undressed."

This time, it was her cheeks that tinged at the implications of the spoken words. Those pink cheeks, along with her blue eyes were intoxicating. I was contemplating saying more inappropriate words, just to see the color deepen. I backed up and leaned against the doorway when she stood up and appraised herself in the mirror as if she were worried the wound would mar her beautiful face. She was still the most beautiful thing I have ever seen.

Her eyes met mine in the mirror. "And your family didn't question that as a werewolf, you had an unconscious female hunter in your arms upon arrival?"

I smiled at her sassiness. "Oh, there were questions. While Lexi was treating you, I informed my brothers of what happened. They were completely aware and supportive of my decision to bring you back here."

She played with the few loose supplies I had left on the counter, still appraising her surroundings. "And your whole family has been tailing my family, trying to get information on us?"

"It sounds a lot worse when you say it like that," I responded.

As if a thought had just entered her mind, her face paled and she pushed past me back into the living area. She looked like she was trying to find and collect her belongings as I followed her in. "I'm sorry," she said. "My family, they're probably looking for me I have to—"

"Henny, after the attack on you, we haven't been able to locate your brother or your father."

She whipped around at my words, her eyes flaring with anger. "Then all the more reason I have to go."

At that point, she must have decided that whatever she was looking for wasn't important because she headed for the door, but I had beaten her there, blocking her view.

"It's not safe for you, Henny. One of your own hunters attacked you last night—"

"Gareth," she ground out.

Ah, so that was Frederiksen. "Okay, well someone who you trusted and have known for years attacked you. Not to mention, he was working with the vampires because they led you right to him. What are you going to do? Are you going to go back to the nest and just stroll in there, avenging what happened?"

Rage was apparent in her eyes. "Yes, that's exactly what I'm going to do, and anyone who tries to stop me is going to get it." She made eye contact at the end of her statement. It was directed at me more than it was directed at the vampires.

I put up my hands to show her that I wasn't going to try to stop her as I slid from the door. She placed her hand on the knob, but I touched it, stopping the action.

"Listen, I get it. If anyone was possibly hurting my family, I would go ballistic. I'm not stopping you, we just need to think for a second. Make a plan before you go charging in. Once you get inside, you might not be sure of what you are going to find. Not to mention, do you even know where you're going? If Gareth was against you, you might not be sure who else is. Let me call my brothers to see if there is any movement from your brother and father. After that, we can figure something out. I promise you, if you don't like what we have to say or the information we give you, you are free to walk out the door." But that was a lie, I wasn't going to let her out of my sight.

"Why are you helping me?" she asked with candor in her eyes.

Because you're my mate. "Because I like your family overseeing the freedom of New Orleans more than vampires," I lied.

She took a minute to contemplate, and then much to my relief, she walked over to the couch and sat down. "Okay," she said.

Okay.

NINE

HENNY

The last twenty-four hours had been a complete whirlwind. So much happened, and I tried to process it all. It felt like one minute, we were out for Reed's birthday, and the next, Gareth betrayed us all. The last thing that I imagined was that I would be sitting in a werewolf's apartment, waiting for his brother to arrive, while we figured out a plan to move forward.

I sat on the couch and stared out to the open window listening to the sounds of city life rushing by. The sun shined, without a cloud in the sky, but it felt off. It mimicked the complete opposite of what I felt. I didn't feel bright and sunny; I felt tumultuous, dark, and gray. Tucking my feet under my knees, I curled into a little ball, resting my face on my hand.

Turning my head, I took in Cole's form as he stood in the kitchen, still on the phone with his family. I watched the way he walked back and forth as he listened to whomever he spoke to on the phone. I couldn't take my eyes off him. Now that he was distracted by something else, I really looked at him. He had an incredibly commanding presence but showed a gentle side as he explained the events of the previous evening to me. For some reason, he genuinely seemed to care about my wellbeing, which was unexpected.

His hair was messily sitting atop his head. Bringing my gaze downward, the collar of his shirt emphasized his strong neck and broad shoulders. The way his bicep curled as he held the phone to his ear made me want to run my fingers down his perfectly smooth skin. His deep, rich voice filtered through the area, and I closed my eyes, taking in the lulling sound it created. Lost in the sound, I hadn't noticed him approach.

"You okay?" he asked calmly, causing me to open my eyes.

"Yes, I'm sorry. I'm just thinking about everything. I'm trying to wrap my head around it all." I let out a long breath. "Trying to make sense of how I feel," I said truthfully bringing my hand up to play with the chain around my neck.

"And what do you feel?" he inquired, folding his arms over his chest and cocking his head to the side. He was staring at me through his thick lashes, and the way he asked the question was sultry.

My body heated instantly. *Stop it, not like that, he's asking about your head.* God, he was beautiful. "It's not that I'm not appreciative for what you've done for me, cause really, I am. I'm still trying to figure out if I should trust you. We're not exactly in the same social groups at school," I tried to joke. "The hunters and werewolves don't exactly care for each other, so why help me?" I asked honestly. I felt he wasn't completely honest with me when he answered last time.

Cole walked over and sat on the couch next to me, straightening his jeans as he rubbed his hands down his thighs. My eyes landed on the strength of his hands. His presence was everywhere; he was overwhelming. Resting his elbows on his knees, he clasped his hands together as if trying to think of what to say.

"That's true, we don't always get along. But Jonah. . .," he started. "My dad always said that when your dad took over our province, it was the best thing that had happened to us so far. He's strict, but he runs things fairly. Your dad treats everyone with an equal amount of respect and dignity. Unfortunately, after last night, his leadership is being challenged. To so openly attack someone, like what had happened to you; nothing good can come of it. Not to mention, I can't imagine that Jonah would condone one of his best hunters working with vampires and attacking his only daughter. Something is brewing, and helping you means figuring out what's in store for all of us." He was right, things seemed to be getting worse.

"Still no word on my father?" I asked holding out a little bit of hope.

"Not much has happened since we brought you here. Bran is on his way, maybe he can provide more information. Liam and Lexi are still out investigating to see if they can find your dad."

I stood up, strolling over to the window to observe the life happening outside. My world was potentially falling apart, but everyone else was going on as normal. Lost in thought, I hadn't heard him approach, but I felt him behind me. I turned around, and we were face to face. Biting my lip, I looked him in the eyes.

"For some reason, I get the feeling I can trust you. That doesn't happen often, but I am usually never wrong, so don't disappoint," I said as I held his eye contact.

This brought a smirk to his face. "Oh yeah? And how do you know you are never wrong?" He took a step closer to me, challenging my statement. A different tone came over him, he seemed flirtatious. This caused my anxiety to rise, and my breath hitched. He'd been so serious thus far, but this seemed almost. . .sensual. His eyes roamed over my face. I shouldn't be feeling this way toward someone, let alone someone I had just met. He did funny things to me. I tried to shake it off.

Encouraged to meet his flirtatious nature, I mustered a little bit of confidence to the surface, matching his coy attitude. He wanted to act sexy? I could play that game too. I licked my lips, which his eyes immediately darted to, and he froze. *Gotcha.* "Because I'm that good at everything I do." *What the heck was I doing?*

As if under a spell, his eyes blazed as he closed the last bit of distance between us. Whatever was about to happen, I would never know because the door to the apartment unlocked and in walked who must have been Cole's brother.

We jumped apart at his entry, and as if he knew what we were doing, a huge smile broke across his face. He was gorgeous. *Did this entire family have flawless genes?* His smile was infectious, and I didn't even realize that I smiled back at him. Cole narrowed his eyes in annoyance.

"You could have fucking knocked," Cole growled as he turned around to face his brother.

"But if I knocked, then I would have missed this incredibly awkward situation we are now all in. Where's the fun in that?" He smiled back at me, placing his hands in his pockets. God, he was so cute.

"Henny, this is Bran; Bran, this is Henny. Bran is my older brother, and definitely the most annoying family member." He offered his hand to me at the introduction. Bran was equal in height to Cole; however, whereas Cole's eyes were a distracting green, Bran's were a warm and calming brown. He was similar to Cole in features only differing by having a smile on his face.

I walked forward while putting a strand of hair behind my ear, suddenly feeling shy from Bran's casual temperament. He definitely didn't care that I was a hunter. I met Bran's outreached hand. "It's nice to meet you," I said curtly, trying to remain civil. I had to remember, I was still in a room with werewolves. Bran smiled back at Cole as he released my hand.

"Hmmm. . .I can see what all the fuss is about," Bran replied.

Cole narrowed his eyes even further.

"What is that supposed to mean?" I asked, but before Bran could answer Cole cut him off.

"Enough, Bran, we need to find out what's going on," Cole stated.

Bran looked at me for a few more seconds and then looked at Cole. "Does she know the background story with us?" Bran inquired, and Cole nodded yes in agreement. Bran turned back to me.

"As Cole was following you, I was appointed to your brother, and Liam was assigned to your dad. Once Cole informed us what happened last night, we went to see if there was any movement from the two of them, or if they even seemed aware of what happened. Last we knew, they were at the manor, so Cassie and I went back there while Liam and Lexi came to you. Once we got to your property, things got a little weird. We shifted to be a little more discrete, which also allowed us to get closer to the woods behind the manor. Once we arrived, there was nothing. It had been deserted. There wasn't a single soul in sight. But when we were leaving, two hunters were exiting the front door when they took a phone call."

I stilled, none of this was making sense. "Did you hear any of the conversation?"

Bran shook his head. "Yes, it was Gareth. He announced to whoever he was speaking with that you, your dad, and Daxon were taken by werewolves. But we heard nothing after that, it's like they're ghosts. After the accusation, Cassie and I thought it would be best if we left to update Liam."

At this statement, Cole swore under his breath and panic took me over. I lost my cool. "What the hell?" I said running my hands over my face, cringing at the situation. "None of this makes sense. I have known Gareth my entire life! We were practically raised together. Why would he do this?" I yelled.

"Do you know where everyone could have gone? The manor acts as your academy also, correct? There had to be more hunters there," Bran asked.

"Not necessarily, if something like that happens, we're told to go into lockdown. There is a tunnel that leads under the estate in the event that we need a quick escape. They could have gotten out that way. It's possible you just didn't hear or see everyone in there," I replied, taking a deep breath. Cole looked at me like he was able to read my mind.

"Don't even think about it," he warned.

"I know that place better than anyone else, there are weapons and safe rooms, if there have been potential threats, someone could have hidden down there," I justified.

"Not happening," he shot back at me.

"I'm not going to sit back and do nothing. Are you forgetting what I am? Where I came from? I know that place like the back of my hand. I will be quick; it won't be long."

"You're injured, and you have a concussion—not to mention it could be a trap," Cole said.

"So, what if it's a trap? This is what I've trained for my entire life, to fight against potential threats. But what sets me apart from other hunters is that I've been trained by the best; therefore, I am the best. I know how to go in undetected. When I go in, I'll be fine. I can even check in afterward, be back by curfew," I said with a hint of sarcasm. I was feeling a little cheeky. I heard Bran laughing in the background, but when I met Cole's eyes again, they held annoyance, probably a product of my defiance.

He took a deep breath. "Fine, but can we think about a plan first? Try and be rational about this? I may not know you very well, but your reckless nature isn't exactly a secret around the city. The last thing I need is you going in there, guns blazing."

I scrunched my nose about the call out but kept my mouth shut because he was probably right. I nodded and was happy that he agreed to at least that. "I have some things stashed around town in the event we needed anything for an emergency. Clothes, a few weapons, a phone. I should probably stop there. I might be able to use the communication to get in touch with Daxon."

Bran stepped forward, but it was Cole who responded. "Yeah, I can take you," he said as he continued to stare at me.

"What?" I asked under his penetrating gaze. I had to look away at the restlessness it caused.

"We're just getting your things right, nothing else? At least until we make a plan?" he questioned.

"Yes, Cole. I promise," I said sweetly as I batted my eyelashes for dramatic effect.

"Okay," he complied. "I get the feeling I can trust you, so don't disappoint," he said as he threw my words back at me.

Bran walked up and looked between the both of us and laughed. "Can we stop for food?" he asked. "I'm kinda hungry," he replied as he headed to the door.

Cole and I took one last look at him as we followed behind.

TEN

COLE

Driving through the streets of New Orleans, I was trying to calm the agitated edge that was running through my veins. I didn't like being in the open like this, it felt exposed. Henny informed me that she had a safety deposit box in a tiny bank on the outskirts of town. Hopefully, she could get in and get whatever she needed, so I could take her back to the safety of my family's cabin. More importantly, she could figure out a way to get in contact with her family.

Everywhere I turned, I was worried there was an unknown force trying to get to her. I didn't like it. Gripping the steering wheel tighter, I chanced a glance at Henny in the rearview mirror. She was staring longingly out the window and had been quiet the entire ride. Bran was showering her with questions, trying to get her to perk up.

I hadn't anticipated the ease that Henny and Bran conversed with. They were discussing information like they were old friends talking about the weather. How would the rest of my family interact with her? If it were anything like with Bran, I was hopeful. Bran shot a joke at her, and she responded with a whimsical laugh.

The last thing I had expected was to feel anything for her. I was just supposed to follow her for a few days to see what they were up to. I never anticipated a mate connection. How was this going to work? Sometimes, there were stories of people fighting it, claiming that mate connections were wrong, but this didn't feel wrong. Even for the few short hours she was around me, it felt so right. Henny broke my train of thought, announcing we needed to make a right at the next street. When our eyes finally connected, she was looking at me as if she had heard my thoughts.

A few minutes later, we pulled up to the curb of the bank where Henny was getting her stuff. I put the car in park to go with her, but she stopped me with a small smile.

"It's a small bank. This is the only exit in the entire building. There is only one room that I get the box out of. I would appreciate a little privacy to change." The thought of her undressing was doing frantic things to my system. I looked over at Bran who just shrugged his shoulders, as if he didn't see a problem with it. It was the middle of the day, there shouldn't be much danger.

"Five minutes," I replied. "We'll be right here."

She opened the door, stopping to look back at me. "Thank you," she said softly as she made her way to the entrance. Both of Bran and I were looking out the window at her retreating form.

"Think she is going to run?" Bran asked.

"Well if she does, thankfully there are two of us to get her," I replied as Bran laughed. I didn't think she would run, my instincts told me she was going to stay with me. *With me.*

"She does seem like a handful," Bran responded lightheartedly.

I blew out a long breath. "You're telling me," I said. I had only known her a few days, and I was already exhausted.

Bran turned and looked at me, growing serious. "She'd be good for you, I can feel it. She is—"

"Bran not right now, dude. Please, I can't think about that now," I lied as I looked out the window. It was the only thing I was thinking about.

"Just think about it, okay?" he asked. "Alright?"

"Alright," I nodded.

Five minutes on the dot, Henny was descending the stairs of the bank looking like a completely different person. Her blonde hair was scooped up into a messy ponytail. The bandages I put on her earlier were now exchanged for small Band-aids. A set of glasses was set on her face, and it looked like a little bit of her color had returned. She looked lighter, more herself, like she hadn't been attacked twenty-four hours earlier. Her tight jeans, flannel shirt, and knee-high boots clung to each portion of her body perfectly as she continued down the stairs. Bran let out a whistle from the seat next to me.

"Man, she really is easy on the eyes, that whole librarian thing she has going on right now," he said.

Only he didn't finish the sentence as I punched him in the arm, annoyed with the attention that he was giving her. Not that it mattered, I wouldn't like the attention any man would give her. It just caused him to laugh.

"Kidding," he said holding his hands up in mock surrender. He knew what the rest of my pack already knew. A mate connection wasn't a fluke. It would be hard to fight it, like fighting fate.

I watched her descend the last few steps as she came back to the vehicle. Opening the door, her blue eyes and soft smile were sending my heart into overdrive. She stumbled into the truck, seemingly as affected as I was. She was flustered as she tried to buckle her seatbelt.

"I was able to grab a few things. Daxon and I have these phones," she held up to show the ancient flip phone. "We have these ready in the event something like this happens. Same thing with my dad, but I'm not getting through to either of them. Have you heard anything further?" she asked with hope.

Bran and I looked at each other, and I put my arm on the back of the passenger seat, looking at her.

"No, I'm sorry," I said, causing her to break eye contact and look out the window. "If you don't mind, we have a family cabin not far from here. It's where we stay a majority of the time. I think it would be useful to touch base with my pack and regroup. Okay?"

I could see the internal struggle that was playing in her eyes. As a hunter, this went against everything that had been ingrained in her training. They were usually the ones in charge. Relinquishing control was not easy, but nothing would happen to her again, I wouldn't allow it. "You'll be safe there, I promise. My family would never hurt you," I answered as she looked between Bran and me.

"Okay," she said quietly with a nod. "But just so you know," she said brightly as she leaned both of her elbows on the back of our seats. "I was top of my class in defensive maneuvers, in case anyone tries to do any funny business."

I smiled, and Bran laughed. "Damn, girl, I kind of want to try something just to see what you've got," Bran responded as he smirked, and Henny sat back in the seat, a glint of satisfaction on her face.

I glared at Bran at the insinuation of him touching her. He knew better, but I was still about to fucking remind him.

I gave her one last look as we pulled away from the curb and a small bit of relief washed over me at her compliance. One thing was certain, never in a million years did I think I would be bringing a hunter to meet my family. I chuckled at the irony.

ELEVEN

HENNY

As we made our way to Cole's cabin, I thought about Daxon and Dad. Cole and Bran casually chatted while my mind was on my family. A few days ago, I didn't think I would be in a situation like this: away from my family and friends, relying on a pack of werewolves to help me. I never thought that Gareth, someone who I was friends with for my entire life, would turn against us. I still couldn't grasp what he was thinking. How could he do that to us? Part of me wanted to find him and beat the shit out of him, but the other part of me wanted to sit him down and get into that brain of his. Nothing that's happened in the last few days makes any sense.

It didn't take long to arrive at Cole's cabin. I had been so lost in thought I hadn't realized that we were in a wooded area, directly in front of a modern, yet rustic, cabin. When the vehicle stopped, Cole and Bran walked out of the car, heading toward their home as they must have done a hundred times before. I slowly stepped out of the truck, taking in the scene in front of me. It wasn't what I expected at all.

The two-story cabin was covered with wood siding, and the pieces were burned with intricate patterns. A wraparound deck led to the back of the house. Two stories of windows faced me, giving way to a screened-in porch on the right. My ears perked as the sound of a babbling brook flowed through the brush to the left of me, the water scurrying into a lake not too far off the property. The tall trees provided shade from the blazing afternoon sun. I looked around, taking in the beautiful sounds of nature. This place was amazing, calm, and serene. Cole stopped, looking back at me.

"This place is breathtaking," I responded, and he gave a soft smile.

"Yeah, when your family business is construction, this is what you get," he said as he held both of his hands out beside him. "Come on," he said, as he gestured at the door, waiting for me to follow.

Something had passed between us, and a sense of ease spread through me. His body language illuminated how much in his element he was. He smiled, and the gesture drew me closer to him. I didn't know why, but at that moment, I had a strong desire to follow Cole wherever he went.

Entering the cabin, the inside was even more beautiful than the outside. The entryway was small but welcoming and larger than expected. The rays of sun shining through the window cast a rainbow glow on the wall that led to the living room, which Bran was now making his way to.

Following his direction, I was met with an open, inviting living room that fostered a beautiful, stone fireplace that sparked a crackling fire, even in the hot month of June. Dark oak lined the floor and brown leather couches surrounded the common area, reminding me of a warm log cabin. An iron chandelier hung from the high ceiling, its lamps cast a soft glow over the seating area. Cole closed the door behind me with a soft click. At the noise, I looked toward the opposite side of the cabin with a stairwell that led down to what must be the basement. A staircase leading to the second floor sat directly in front of me. I looked at him, and he gestured to the living area that I admired. Trying to remember my formal training, I turned to Cole.

"Um," I stammered. "Five members in your pack, correct?" I asked trying to flip my mind to all the times my dad went over respectful introductions, instantly regretting not paying more attention to his lessons. Cole nodded.

"It's just us. Although we do have members of different packs coming and going at any given time. As I said, the pack from Atlanta visits a lot, but most of the time, it's just me, Bran, Cassandra, Liam, and Lexi."

"And Liam, he's your Alpha?" I continued.

Cole looked at me like he was trying to find the right words when I noticed figures taking form behind me in the living room. I turned and came face to face with his family. The only guy I haven't met, Liam, was a bit shorter and stockier than the two brothers. He nodded his head respectfully in my direction. The younger of the two women came bounding forward, a warm smile lighting up her face, radiating bubbly energy. The other brunette, who seemed more reserved, offered a small smile as she walked to Liam's side. Cole came up from behind me, offering introductions.

"Henny, these are my siblings, Liam and Cassandra. This is Lexi, Liam's mate." Both Liam and Lexi said a curt hello and nodded in my direction. Cassie, who still beamed at me, looked like she was going to run and give me a hug, but as a warning, Cole's glare stopped her.

Both women were brunettes; Lexi was tall and lean whereas Cassie looked short and petite. Lexi's tall frame towered over Cassie, who was closer to my height. Both girls had shining brown hair and almond-shaped eyes. A sprinkle of freckles surrounded Cassie's face, which made her look the youngest of the bunch.

"Wow! Oh, you're so pretty!" Cassie stated, still smiling at me. Then her eyes widened like she hadn't meant to say what had come out of her mouth. I liked her already.

"Cassie, jeez. You only just met her, don't be weird," Cole remarked.

Cassie looked at me like she was afraid she had said something wrong.

"Don't worry, I prefer smiling and compliments to brooding," I replied as I slid my eyes toward Cole.

"Ha! Ain't that the truth?" Bran said as he joined the rest of us.

Cassie laughed, and it looked like Lexi was suppressing a smile.

Liam interrupted my thoughts. "Henrietta, you've had quite the few days. We have spare bedrooms; why don't you go get settled, and then when you're ready, you can come back downstairs, and we can talk about what we know. Lexi said that she has some extra clothes that you can wear until we get things figured out."

I nodded. "Thank you, everyone, I appreciate the help."

Everyone gave reassuring smiles as Cole came into my line of vision. "The bigger rooms are upstairs, I'll take you to the one that has the bathroom attached."

I followed Cole as he made his way to the room which would be my temporary home, admiring the oak woodwork as I ascended to the second floor. He was silent as he led the way. Taking a right at the top of the stairs, he stopped in front of the door at the end of the hallway.

The room was just as beautiful as the rest of the house. High ceilings made the room look open and spacious, and windows lined three of the four walls in the bedroom. The only wall that did not have windows was the wall the housed a king-sized four-poster bed, complete with white twinkle lights hanging from the banisters. The bedspread was done in a flannel, checkered pattern, matching the two love seats that sat in the front corners of the room overlooking the forest. There was a door on the other side of the bed leading to the bathroom. The windows were open, casting a light breeze through the room. I went to the window, breathing in the open air. Everything was incredibly peaceful. I looked further, taking in the vast size of the sparkling lake that looked like tiny diamonds rested on top of it. Toward the bottom of the house, there was a stone patio with a firepit in the middle directly in front of the doors of a walkout basement. I looked at him and smiled.

"It appears your family has a future in interior design. This place is very charming," I said.

"Unfortunately, I can't take credit. That's Lexi's specialty." Cole smiled.

Taking in the rest of the room, I was lost in my thoughts for a few minutes when I turned around to ask Cole a question. I was met with his penetrating gaze. It was so fierce, it felt like those green eyes read every thought in my mind. The intensity of his gaze caught me off guard, and I forgot what I was going to say. My mind once again grew fuzzy.

He stood in the doorway with his arms folded over his muscular chest. It only accentuated his biceps, which really highlighted how strong he looked. My mind floated to how strong his arms would feel when wrapped around me. *Stop it!* I reprimanded myself.

"You were going to ask something?" Cole interrupted my thoughts, bringing me back to the present.

He had definitely caught me ogling that time, and he knew it as he came further into the room with a newfound swagger. He played with the edge of the quilt on the bed, meeting my eyes again.

"I, uh, ummmm," I said still not able to get the words out. "I'm sure it will come to me," I said as he nodded, smirking.

"The bathroom is right through that doorway, and I believe it is stocked with everything that you need. There should also be towels in there, and I'll make sure Lexi brings you some more clothes to wear. Are you hungry?"

As if hearing his question, my stomach growled loudly, and I put my hand against it. Cole laughed.

"A little," I replied, embarrassed at the perfectly normal function.

"I think Lexi is making something to eat anyway. It should be ready by the time you're done."

I stood there staring at him. *Stop being creepy.*

"Okay, well, my room is next door if you need anything," he said as he turned to go into the hallway.

"I thought you lived at the studio apartment? I didn't realize that you lived here, too."

He leaned against the banister of the poster bed. "Is it a problem for you that I'm next door?" he asked as he cocked an eyebrow, suddenly being playful. The expression on his face was gorgeous.

"No, I'm sorry, I was just wondering. I appreciate all the help." I made my way to the bathroom so that I wouldn't get caught up in those captivating eyes again. I took one last look at him before I went in. I heard him walk out the door, shutting it behind him.

After what felt like hours in a hot shower, I used the time to clear my head and think of how I was going to liberate Dax and Dad. I constructed a plan of action to go out looking for them. My temples felt a little better, but they were tender to the touch. Stepping out of the shower, I inhaled the warm steam and wrapped myself in a fluffy cotton towel. Wiping the mirror, I took in my appearance and had to admit, I'd seen better days. Taking my time putting on fresh clothes, I walked back into the room when I noticed Lexi placing more blankets on the bed for me. She turned around and smiled.

"Do you feel better?" she asked.

I nodded.

"And you're comfortable?" she added, and I nodded again. "I'm glad," she responded once more. She must have thought that I wanted to be alone because she turned around to walk out of the room. I couldn't stop the question that came out of my mouth.

"Why are you helping me?" I sounded harsher than I intended, and I closed my eyes and sighed at the way the question sounded. "I'm sorry, I didn't mean for it to come out like that, to sound rude. It's just hunters and werewolves don't exactly get along or have the best relationship. I get why Cole is helping me, but the rest of you have taken me in and have offered to help, no questions asked. If this were the other way around, I regret to say that the hospitality you would experience at the hands of my people may not be as kind."

Lexi smiled like she was reliving an inside joke. She walked over to the bed and softly sat on the corner. While I still felt a little uncomfortable because I had only just met her, I stood by the bathroom door and leaned against the doorframe.

"There is one thing about werewolves that you might be familiar with, and that is we are fiercely protective of those who are our own or part of our pack. We treat each other like family. When Liam and I received the call from Cole that he found you that night, he sounded frantic. We knew we needed to help. It's who we are. There were no questions asked. Also, you don't exactly turn down an Alpha's command," she replied with a smile.

My head snapped up at the words she just said. *Wait, what?* "Cole is your pack's Alpha?" I asked, shocked. I automatically assumed it was Liam as he was the oldest and seemingly more in command. It's no wonder Cole hesitated in the entryway. Realization dawned on Lexi's face that I didn't yet know this information and her eyes widened.

"It's okay, Lexi," Cole said from the doorway looking just as delicious as he did earlier. *Damn, I was hoping that feeling would go away.* "I was going to share that information with Henny once she was more comfortable."

Our eyes connected, and something passed between us. I couldn't look away. The pull I had toward him was getting stronger and stronger. For the first time in my life, there was something I didn't have any control over, and it made me uneasy. Lexi had stood, looking back at me. She smiled as she walked out of the room.

"Come on, let's go for a walk. We'll talk," he said.

As if on autopilot, my body floated over to his, immediately obeying his command. He gave me a small smirk that made me tingle in all sorts of places. *Oh crap, this so isn't good.*

TWELVE

COLE

It was nice being outside with Henny. At least with the fresh air, I could think a little better as her presence was everywhere. While she was taking a shower, I went downstairs with my family to see what the new updates were. They weren't good. There was still no news on Jonah or Daxon. As far as we could tell, they disappeared off the face of the planet. When vampires are involved, the options are minimal. Two things typically happen as a result of that, individuals are either drained or turned. I was hoping it was neither. This information was going to be hard for Henny, and I had finally gotten her to calm down. This would send her into an even further panic.

Once we were outside, we quietly walked deeper into the forest. Glancing out of the corner of my eye, she had seemed to relax as she was taking in the surroundings. This place did that to you. I didn't think it was possible, but she looked even more beautiful. We walked for a while, and it was Henny who broke the reprieve.

"It's beautiful out here. How long have you guys lived here?" she asked.

"It's been a while, as long as I can remember. My mother loved the lake and everything surrounding it. My father wanted to find a place for her that she loved, but where she was protected. The way our cabin is placed does just that."

"What happened to your parents? If you don't mind me asking?" she asked as we kept walking.

I was hesitant to answer as I knew where her mind was going. She was thinking something happened to her family.

It took me a second to answer. I hadn't talked about them for a while. It was hard still getting over what happened. It still brought up memories that I was Alpha and Liam wasn't. I was still getting used to the fact that the lives of my family were in my hands.

"I'm sorry, if it's hard to talk about, you don't have to answer," she said.

I could read the sympathy on her face. She knew how it felt. I had known from the information Liam had given to me that her mom had passed shortly after her and her brother were born, so she recognized the loss.

"No, it's okay. It's just been a while since I've talked about them," I answered. We continued walking, almost reaching the lake when the breeze picked up, almost as if a sign that my parents were with us. I smiled. My mother would have loved Henny. There would have been no judgment that she wasn't one of us. In her eyes, we were all the same.

"We were at a gathering one night with a few other packs. It was a celebration for one of the neighboring Alpha's newly-mated son. His dad had been close to mine. Everything was fine until a female member came tearing out of the woods, screaming for help. Something about vampires and hunters just on the outskirts of the property. Naturally, my brothers and I, along with my father went to check it out. I noticed my mother was following. There was a thing about my mother, you never told her no."

This caused a smile so bright on Henny's face that my heart swelled. I continued.

"At first, my father argued, but he knew that he couldn't stop her. Once that woman had made up that mind, there was no resisting her. Not only was her mate going into danger but so were her babies. We shifted. My mom and dad went one way, and my brothers and I went another. I've never seen two mated wolves as connected as my parents were. Wherever one went, the other followed, like magnets. That was the last time I saw them alive. We never really found out what happened. We just know that when we found them, they were together," I looked away from her, feeling choked up about the memory.

Henny tilted her head to the side empathizing with my feelings. "I'm sorry," she said as she gently touched my forearm. "She sounds like an exceptional lady. Fearless and loyal to those she loves. Those are admirable traits. I would have liked to meet her." The way she was talking about my mother only made me even more attracted to her, and the mate connection was sealing even further.

"She was exceptional and fearless. But man, stubborn as all hell."

This generated the sweetest sounding laugh from Henny, causing her to smile even brighter.

"It reminds me of someone I just met," I said as my eyes locked with hers.

Meeting my gaze, Henny's cheeks flushed. I took a step closer, trying to capture every bit of this moment and enjoying the space of just the two of us. My closeness made the pink blush deepen further. My mind was imagining the things I could do to keep that color on her cheeks, and I wondered what other parts of her body I could make flush.

"Hey guys!" Cassie stated as she came out of the clearing.

I straightened and Henny jumped at my sister's appearance. Cassie had an impressively large grin on her face as she read the situation.

"Henny, big baby Bran wanted to go swimming. We hope it's okay that we are meeting out here," Cassie stated as she ran to the lake, jumping into the water.

A shirtless Bran came into view. "Actually, maybe I just wanted Henny to see my super voluptuous bod," he said as he jumped into the water, too.

When he broke the water's surface, I whipped a baseball-sized rock at his head, glaring at him for the comment. I looked over at Henny, who was smiling.

"So, have you guys heard anything?" Henny asked my brother and sister as she walked over to sit on a large rock near the edge of the lake.

Cassie and Bran swam right up to the rock where Henny was sitting, and I sat on the edge right beside her. I knew everything they were about to say.

"There have been some developments," Liam said as he made his way into the clearing, Henny turning toward him. "It's literally like they have vanished off the map. Not only haven't we been able to locate your father or brother, but we haven't heard a sound from Gareth. It's like he has disappeared with them. We reached out to a few trusted friends. Word is getting around that the four of you are missing. Gossip is that you had been killed by a rogue pack of werewolves. That's not good for anyone. It's not good for the werewolves because the hunters will be out for blood, and that's not good for the hunters because the werewolves will think it's a setup."

Henny was silent beside me. "Well, that can be easily fixed. I will just let everyone know that I'm fine when I go back to check out the manor."

Liam and I were hesitant at that. We were worried that was what Gareth was counting on.

"Henny," I said when she turned to me.

Her serious gaze looked even bluer with the water reflecting nearby.

"We think that's what Gareth wants you to do. We think that he is trying to draw you out. With you being alive, it's a liability for him. If word gets out about what he's done, it would induce chaos."

She let out a sigh as she got up and walked toward the edge of the lake. She picked up a stone and skipped it into the water. Even though she seemed distressed, she looked heavenly with her blonde hair blowing gently in the wind. She was staring out into the horizon with her arms gently crossed over her chest. She turned around, and a look of sadness marred her features. "It's possible. It appears I don't even know who he is anymore," she took a deep breath and continued. "So, what should we do now? I don't know if I can trust anyone I would reach out to." The conversation was directed at my family, but Henny's eyes were on me.

I had an idea. It wasn't a great one, but it was something. "You still have a contact for Jackson?" I asked Liam, and he nodded. "Make the call."

I was looking at Henny and getting ready to do something that I really didn't want to do, but it didn't matter, I would do anything to help her.

THIRTEEN

HENNY

After we left the lake, Cole and Liam constructed plans to figure out our next point of contact. Apparently, they were familiar with a member of another pack named Jackson. They weren't particularly fond of him as he did a lot of backhanded dealings; however, Cole felt strongly that if someone knew any further information, it would be him.

After the lake, I went upstairs, back to the room that had been lent to me. I was deep in thought when there was a knock at the door. I walked over to open it and found Cole standing in the doorway, and I opened it further to welcome him in. As he entered my room, he went over to stand by the window. He turned around and sat on the edge of the sill, resting his hands on his knees.

"We were able to get a hold of the beta of Jackson's pack, but they won't meet us halfway, we have to go to the MC club to meet with them."

"Do you think going all the way out there could be dangerous?" I asked, but Cole shook his head.

"He's usually like this; he always has to be in control," he said as he rolled his eyes. "We have to get a few things first, so we'll head out tomorrow morning. I'll let you know when we're leaving."

"Okay, what am I going to need to bring?" I asked. I wanted to leave now, I was ready. We've had nothing to go on thus far so this was at least a start.

Cole's eyebrows creased. "What do you mean? Henny, you're not going. You're going to stay here with Lexi and Cassie. They will be able to take care of you," he replied.

"You're kidding, right?" I said as I narrowed my eyes at him.

He stood up and crossed his arms over his chest. "No, I'm not kidding, these guys are bullies. They will love nothing more than to push you around. Not to mention you're gorgeous. I don't want to have to be fighting these guys off of you while I'm trying to uncover information."

My heart fluttered a little. *He thinks I'm gorgeous?* Wait, that was beside the point. I was mad they were going to leave me behind. I chuckled, crossing my own arms in return. "The hell I'm not going. This is my family we are talking about here, and you just want me to sit at home on my ass?" I registered the look of shock on his face from calling his place my home and panic took over. "I mean not my home, *home.* But like at home. A house of some sort. A place where people live. . .ish." *God, shut up Henny!* I clamped my mouth shut immediately.

"Are you done?" he smirked. Him thinking this situation was funny only made me more irritated.

"Cole, I'm going. This could be the first lead that we have. There is no way that you cannot let me in."

"And what if this is dangerous? Then what?" he asked.

"Yeah, well I'm not afraid of a few bullies, I am more than capable of taking care of myself."

He was calculating like he waged an internal battle in his head.

"I mean, I guess I could figure out a way to go on my own," I started.

He sighed, accepting defeat. "Alright, fine. But Henny, these werewolves are not like my family. They are rude and crass, and they don't follow the rules. This is a different environment than what you are used to. If you go, you have to do things our way. You have to listen to me, do you understand?"

"I understand," I answered, and he gave me a pointed look. "I said okay!" I replied. I wasn't going to push my luck, I was just happy that he agreed. I thought that I was going to have to push a lot harder than that.

He continued to sit on the windowsill watching me. Suddenly feeling shy, I started playing with the edge of my shirt. Risking a look back up at him, I took in his long lashes, the curve of his lips, and his deep, rich scent. I bit my lip to distract myself from the not-so-appropriate things I thought right then. My hand reached up to play furiously with my necklace.

"Okay," he said. "I need to make a few more phone calls. I'll let you know when we find out more information," he said as I nodded in agreement.

I felt the exhaustion kicking in. It had been a rough couple of days, and it started to catch up with me. My temples pounded as well. I didn't acknowledge any of that because I didn't want to give Cole another reason to keep me back. He took one last look at me, then nodded and left the room. I sat on the bed, exhaling a deep breath, feeling the full weight of the situation. Even though it wasn't nightfall, I changed into the pajamas that Lexi offered and tried to lie down to calm my thoughts. As the quiet descended, it made my mind go to deep and dark places. I didn't hear from Cole the rest of the night. After what finally felt like hours of tossing and turning, my eyes closed as they succumbed to the slumber.

I shot up in the bed, the nightmare I just had sent adrenaline coursing through my veins. My chest compressed from the panic. Replaying the dream, images of vampires attacking Daxon and my dad flooded my mind, causing tears to prick my eyes. It felt so vivid and real. It felt like fate was toying with me; no matter what I did, I couldn't get to them now. Dragging my eyes to the windows, the outside was shrouded in darkness now. The only thing that broke the silence of the night was my rapid breathing.

I tried to steady my breath, which came out in short pants. I wiped a thin layer of sweat from the back of my neck as fear emanated inside me. Almost as instantly as I woke, the bedroom door flew open, and Cole stood in the doorway with a look of concern. All I could do was stare at him with a mirrored look of worry on my face. After determining there was no further threat, his eyes softened as he understood my panic. Softly walking into my room, he sat on the edge of the bed, taking my trembling hands in one of his. He used his other hand to take my chin with his finger, turning my face to his. I blinked away the tears once again, and he moved his finger to caress my cheek. It felt like time stood still as we sat there staring at one another. He moved his hand and ran it in a soothing motion up and down my back. Feeling defeated, I leaned forward to rest my forehead against his collarbone, and he tightened his hold, projecting calm over me. Turning his head to face mine, he brought his other hand up and ran his fingers through my hair.

"It's going to be okay," he said. "You're going to be okay," he whispered as he rubbed my back, lulling me back into a fitful sleep.

The next day, the four of us headed north of New Orleans. I remained quiet most of the morning, the after effects of my nightmare still lingering. Liam and Cole discussed that Jackson really wasn't on a good or bad side, but he was on the "Jackson" side, meaning whatever side benefit him the most. It was only when Jackson's guys had a run-in with the vampires did Gareth's name surface. I was trying to listen to their conversation, but I couldn't concentrate long enough to comprehend the words. Bran kept trying to pull me out of my silent reprieve, and Cole turned back to look at me.

"Henny, listen, these guys are a pain in the ass. They are going to try and bait you, and say things to piss you off only to get a rise out of you. I'm begging you not to react. We didn't mention that you're a hunter because that would just add fuel to the fire, but they'll probably be able to sense that you're different. If you say something that could start a fight with a full-blown werewolf, it's going to draw attention, and not the good kind. So please, just stay quiet. Is that something that you can do?"

It was Bran who spoke up next. "I, for one, would actually love to see her whoop everyone's ass, those guys deserve it. Maybe beating some sense into them would be helpful," he said as he winked at me.

I couldn't help but release a smile. When I turned back to look at Cole, he didn't seem amused.

"I'm serious, Henny. Please?"

"Alright. I will try, but I'm not making any promises. These guys sound like—"

Cole let out a sigh and wiped his hands over his face. "Damnit Henny, please," was all he said as a look of frustration marred his beautiful face. I didn't like that I was the one who had caused it.

"Alright, I won't say anything," I answered holding up my fingers in a scout's honor position.

When we had pulled up to the club, I wasn't expecting the dumpy hole-in-the-wall feel that it projected. There were no windows on either the first or second stories, and the only glass was in the door leading to the entrance. Cole, Liam, and I exited from the vehicle and made our way toward the bar. Bran came in behind us. They didn't even acknowledge the mean looking bouncer eyeing us with curiosity. We didn't stand out that much, did we? The guys were dressed casually in flannels and jeans, and I wore black leggings, black knee-high boots, and a black tank top covered by a thin denim jacket. Even though the place looked remotely empty from the outside, there were a lot of people around the tables and at the bar. A few groups played pool toward the back. As it grew later in the evening, it became busier.

Cole stopped as he looked around. He then made eyes with a bartender who nodded toward the stairway leading to the second story offices. We walked that way and were followed by different sets of eyes through the bar. It was obvious that we were expected. The bar was filled with mostly men, but the women that were present seemed to be vying for their attention. The looks that I received unsettled me. There were a lot more werewolves in here than I expected. As if sensing my discontent, Cole put his hand on my lower back and guided me to the stairs. "Please stay close to me and remember what I said. And whatever you do, do *not* drink anything," he said and then stopped in his tracks, turning me to him. "Do you understand?"

"What do you mean do not drink—" my face masked with confusion as Cole cut me off.

"Henny, please, just trust me on this one," he gave me a pleading look, and I nodded. Up the stairs, there was a small hallway with a few doors on each side. At the end of the hall, two werewolves stood outside an office, looking intimidating as hell.

As we made our way to the end of the hallway, the blond-haired man looked at Cole. "Martin," he acknowledged. He turned his eyes on me, blatantly looking me up and down, which brought an unwelcome slithering sensation to my skin. "And guest," he finished as he licked his lips.

Cole stepped in front of me, anger radiating off him. The bouncer turned back to Cole, clearly annoyed at Cole's protective nature.

"What can I do for you?" he asked as if he didn't know what we were doing there.

"Don't bullshit me, Axel. You know we are here to see Jackson," Cole said, standing a little taller.

"That's true," he agreed. "But there was no agreement that this sweet little thing would be joining you for the meeting. She'll have to wait downstairs," Axel responded tightlipped.

"Yeah, that's not happening. She stays with us," Cole replied.

Axel only laughed. "Then you're not seeing Jackson. You know he's very particular about who he meets with, and I'm pretty sure he didn't agree to the hunter joining in on the fun. Your brothers only. But, I'm sure if she heads downstairs, she'll be taken care of," Axel answered as he licked his lips again.

Slimeball. Growing anxious that Jackson would refuse to see Cole, I responded. "Cole, it's fine. I can go downstairs," I said and made my way to the stairs. Cole grabbed my arm.

"Henny, I said you stay with me," he stated with a severe look in his eyes.

"Then you might as well leave because Jackson won't see you with anyone else," Axel noted.

"I can stay with her," Bran suggested.

Cole seemed to take a few seconds to contemplate when he looked at Liam who nodded in agreement. His hand slid down my arm, and our fingertips touched, causing goosebumps all over my body. His eyes bored into mine.

"Do NOT drink anything," he said as he looked over my shoulder at Bran. "Do not take your fucking eyes off of her. You got it?" Cole snarled.

"Relax, we'll be fine," Bran stated confidently.

Cole turned back to Axel as he opened the door. With one last look at me, Cole and Liam entered the office, the door closing behind them.

I turned to Bran. "How did they know I was a hunter? I thought that wasn't exactly something that you can sense? I thought it was more of a human-type thing?" I questioned.

Bran laughed. "No offense darling, but you don't exactly give off the girl next door vibe. Not to mention, some of the stronger Alpha's have the ability to sense these things. Just like Cole was able to sense you. Come on, let's go downstairs and hide in a corner so you don't cause any trouble."

I rolled my eyes as I followed him downstairs. The atmosphere was completely different than it was a few minutes ago. When we were upstairs, the music got a little louder, and it was far more seductive than it was earlier. The women were vying for the men's attention earlier, but now they stepped it up a notch. Many of them were draped all over the patrons in the bar. Waving my hand in front of my face, the air felt so much thicker and smelled of. . .flowers? *Weird.* Not what I was expecting from a werewolf motorcycle bar. We went to one of the hidden corner tables. It only took seconds before two blonde women immediately flocked to Bran. *Figures.* They acted like I didn't even exist; however, Bran nervously turned my way every few seconds to make sure that I was still within eyesight. I was antsy as this was taking a little longer than expected. One more woman joined us, and I noticed that it felt like the air grew warmer and denser.

Tapping my fingers on the table in impatience, I felt my skin flush. Even after slipping off my jacket, I needed to go to the bathroom to splash some water on my face to cool my skin. Bran was now completely distracted by his entourage, and he ran his finger up one of the blondes' arms. I looked behind him and noticed the bathroom door. It was just a few steps, I would be fine. Sliding out of the booth, a slight wave of dizziness came over me. I shook it off and kept walking to the bathroom. Splashing water on my face seemed to do nothing to ease the flush on my skin. As I exited the bathroom, the lights dimmed even further, and the music was more provocative. My heart pounded in my chest.

Making my way back to the table, Bran now full-fledged danced with the women. I rolled my eyes at how easily I was forgotten. Not that I cared, but it made me smile a little at how much of a ladies' man he was. He seemed so free, and I was a little jealous of his carefree nature. As I watched him, I felt my own body sway to the beat, the music growing more enticing as I moved my body more and more. The cloudiness in my head took over.

As if on autopilot, I made my way to the crowded dance floor, relinquishing myself to the beat. The air was heavy due to all the people around, and the temperature of this place reached an all-time high.

Sweat dripped down my neck. I let my fingers run through my hair as I lifted it off my neck, and I continued to sway seductively. It was like an unknown force had taken over my body.

The more I swayed, the sexier I felt. The music and the bass were pounding through my core, and I couldn't help but move like I was the only person in the room. I don't know how or why, but next thing I knew I ended up on the bar with a few other girls. I continued to dance like I didn't care who watched. I moved my body to the rhythm as guys were flooding to the bar area. It made my inner vixen smile. If they wanted a show, I was going to give it to them.

I played with the thin straps of my tank as I moved my hands down my body and over my thighs. *Stop.* A voice said inside my head, but I was too in tune with the music to listen. *You better stop what you're doing.* The crowd surrounding me and the other girls grew larger. I observed the tall, broad men who encircled us, and damn, they were gorgeous. A few of them grabbed the hands of other girls as they led them off the bar, but I was perfectly content dancing by myself. Sweat dripped down my cleavage as I continued to dance seductively.

A werewolf approached me with blond hair and golden eyes that would make any girl go weak in the knees. Making eye contact with me, he smiled.

"Why don't you come down from there, and you can show me a little more closely what types of moves you have?" he said flirtatiously. He held out his hand to help me off the bar. The fuzziness in my head made me giddy, and I giggled.

"I'm good," I answered back as I continued to dance.

His eyes never left my body, but as if a switch was flipped, I now felt like I was overheating. He must have noticed.

"Then at least let me get you some water to cool off for a minute. You can take a break, and then get right back up there," he said, holding his hand out for me once more.

I now noticed that his arms were covered in tattooed sleeves with a small lip ring glinting off the reflection of the dim lights. Water did sound amazing, and why is it so hot in here?

"Okay, but just for a few minutes," I responded, the dizziness returning. As I reached out to take his hand and hop off the bar, my eyes connected with a pair of shockingly green, glowing eyes. They were stunning. Our eyes remain connected, and the look on his face was nothing less than thunderous rage. The anger in his eyes caught me off guard, so I missed my footing and stumbled off the bar. Seeing Cole was like a shock to the system, and I tried to shake off what I felt.

I heard a warm chuckle from the blond-haired guy who caught me. "Perhaps we need to have a seat," he said as he pulled me rather close. The next thing I knew, his lips were at my ear. "I know just the place where the two of us can rest," he whispered bewitchingly.

Before I met his eyes, he was shoved out of the way, and Cole's large frame stood in front of me with his back blocking me from the blond man.

"That's enough, Archer. Take a walk, she's off limits," Cole sneered.

Archer stood up a little straighter to match Cole's intimidating form. "I don't think so, Martin. You can tell just as strongly as I can that she's not off limits to anyone, *yet*," Archer spat out with a cocky grin on his face. I felt the anger roll off Cole in waves. I realized what was going on, and the blazing temperature now rapidly descended. It felt like the walls were closing in. Not knowing where they came from, Bran and Liam were behind me, practically boxing me in. Bran ran a hand over his face.

As if Cole could get any more intimidating, he stepped toward Archer. His voice was nothing but a whisper, but it spewed venom.

"I SAID NO," he replied with a deadly stare as he started to roll his neck from side to side and the veins in his forearms tightened. Archer chuckled, completely ignoring Cole as he licked his lips and made his way back to me. Cole was too fast, though. Right as Archer was about to pass him, Cole punched him directly in the face. Whatever was left of Cole's resolve dissipated.

"She is fucking mine. Do you understand me?" Cole shouted as he grabbed the front of Archer's shirt, holding him up. He started to tumble from the shock he just received. Where there was once a cocky attitude, fear shown in Archer's eyes as he nodded to Cole. Cole looked into the eyes of the crowd that had now collected. "Did everyone hear that?" he shouted. "She's mine!"

Cole turned to meet my eyes when my vision started to blur. *Wait, did I drink anything?* It felt like I had too many drinks as nausea came over me. The last half hour wasn't exactly clear. Registering my thoughts, Cole's beautiful green eyes were the last thing I saw before my knees gave out and I fell.

FOURTEEN

COLE

I ran to grab Henny as she crashed to the floor. This went a lot worse than I was expecting, thanks to Bran for thinking with his dick instead of his brain. I was going to kill him.

The meeting seemed to be going smoothly upstairs, and we were exchanging information. Jackson had heard some talk that there was a rouge hunter who was planning on taking different packs down in the area. The information was given to them by a vampire they had captured. I didn't even want to think about what they did to get the monster to talk. With Jonah potentially out of the way, along with his best hunters, that meant the Southern Province would be a free for all. If they were planning on this kind of takeover, then that meant that Henny was in more danger than we had originally thought.

When one of Jackson's security guards opened the door, the strongest scent hit my nose. It was highly enticing and smelled exactly like. . .Henny? Liam whipped his head in my direction as his eyes widened, picking up on my thoughts.

A pheromone mixture was floating through the building. This immediately put me on fucking edge. Pheromones enhanced the experience between two werewolves. It was like a drug to us. Somehow, Jackson was able to capture its essence, it's one of the things he sold under the table.

"Did you dissolve the elixir through the air vents?" Liam questioned, and it sent my anger through the roof. *How did he know that?*

"What the fuck is going on here?" I snarled as Liam took a step closer to Jackson.

"Fucking calm down, Martin, I'm just trying to have a little fun for my men. They work hard they deserve a little treat. We are getting close to a full moon," Jackson said smugly as he folded his arms over his chest.

My mind instantly went to Henny. She wasn't a supernatural per se, so it shouldn't affect her like it does us, but I needed to get to her. Now.

"Plus, I'm sure that sweet little hunter you brought in here will be the sweetest treat of all. Mmm those hips and that tiny little waist," he replied as I charged at him. Liam was holding me back.

"Cole, it's not worth it. We have to get out of here." This dissolved any progress that we were making with Jackson as an ally.

I turned around looking directly into Jackson's eyes. "I swear to God, if one of your men touched a hair on her head, I will fucking kill him." I didn't wait for Jackson's response as I threw open the door and raced down the stairs. Liam was following directly behind me.

Once I reached the first floor, I searched for any signs of Bran or Henny. I prayed to God that Bran would have picked up on what was happening and would have taken her outside. Liam slapped me on the arm and pointed in the direction of a dark booth in the corner, which housed my brother and two extremely attractive women. Henny was nowhere in sight.

I looked at my brother. "You go grab Bran and get him the fuck out of here while I find Henny."

Liam nodded and made his way to our brother. I pushed through the now compacted bar looking in every direction for her. Looking upward toward the figures on the bar, I spotted Henny. My body was frozen at the way she was running her hands all over her body. I closed my eyes to clear my head, trying to expel the sensual feelings that were now creeping into my body. The fragrance was so much thicker down here. Opening my eyes, my gaze went to her once more, and man, she looked so fucking sexy. The effects of the elixir caused whoever took it to be become flushed with heat, and in some cases, highly aroused. Judging by the way she was dancing, she was experiencing both. That brought salacious things into my mind. But these elixirs were typically charmed for supernaturals. Hunters were essentially humans, so how was this happening? I couldn't take my eyes off her and was experiencing the effects that I had been trying to hide. Elixir or no elixir, I realized how much I wanted and needed her. It was clear, she was mine.

No sooner than the thought escaped my mind, Archer Marx floated over to her, trying to lower her body down to his. Judging by the way she practically fell into his arms, her eyes fluttering shut, she might have gone with him. Was she feeling that way because of him or because of what was floating through the air? It took me no time to get over to her.

The second I reached them, I was seething at the thought of his hands touching her. Henny looked at me with wide, clouded eyes. Having the audacity to challenge me, I had to lay Archer's ass out.

I went to catch Henny as she was falling to the ground. I scooped her up in my arms and turned around to meet both of my brothers' gazes. Liam looked pissed, and Bran looked scared, probably because he realized what happened or what could have happened. He should have been scared of what I was going to do to him. I heard my name called from the balcony.

"Martin, I'm giving you three seconds to get your fucking brothers and that hunter out of this bar before I let my boys loose on you."

As I looked at the scene before me, a few of Archer's buddies stared back. I would have fought every last one of them to keep them from touching Henny.

"Time to go," Liam whispered in my ear as he came up behind me. He didn't have to tell me twice.

We headed straight for the door and right to the truck once we were outside. Henny was barely conscious, slurring her words and giggling. Ugh. I couldn't control my anger at what they did at the bar; what they did to her. It wasn't her fault, but there was another matter to attend to first.

"Wait," I said. Both of my brothers stopping to question me. I turned to Liam, gently transferring Henny into his arms. When I turned to face Bran, he knew what was going to happen. He put his palms up in shock as his eyes widened.

"Dude, let me explain," he started to say as he was backing up.

"Don't fucking care," I responded. I didn't even register my fist flying toward his face until it connected with his cheekbone, just under his right eye. Within seconds, his ass was on the ground. I stepped over him, grabbing the front of his shirt and forcing him to look at me. "What the fuck were you thinking? Do you fucking know what could have happened to her if Liam and I hadn't made it downstairs when we did? Where the fuck would she be right now?" I shouted, pushing him further into the gravel. My anger was building, and I felt Liam pull me off Bran, who was sporting an already blackened eye. He would get over it. At the rate in which we healed, it would probably be fine by the time we got home.

"Calm down, Cole. It's too much. This is too much," Liam said, sounding very much like our father at that moment. It snapped me out of my anger. I let go of Bran's shirt, taking deep breaths, trying to control my rage. He was right. While Bran should have been watching over Henny, this ultimately wasn't his fault.

"Cole, dude, I'm sorry, I don't know what came over me. It's like she was sitting right there and then next thing I know, she wasn't there anymore. I would never want anything to happen to her," Bran responded.

I tried to steady my breathing and calm down. If I didn't relax, I was going to shift. It was only then that I noticed that Henny was no longer in Liam's arms because he was holding me back. I looked back, and she was gently tucked in the back seat of the truck, her wide blue eyes watching me.

"Let's fucking go!" I shouted as I climbed in the back of the truck with Henny, slamming the door shut. Her skin still looked pale, and a light layer of sweat was coating her forehead. She looked at me with a daze and then gave a small smile. She was completely out of it, but she never broke eye contact. I took a loose piece of hair from her ponytail and placed it behind her ear as I ran my knuckles down her neck. She closed her eyes in satisfaction. I grabbed a t-shirt that was laying in the back and wetted it with a water bottle, patting it against her forehead. She scrunched her nose and swatted the wet cloth away. I didn't fight her, there was no use after what was coursing through her body right now.

After a silent ride home, we pulled up to the cabin, and I turned to help Henny out of the truck. While she was stepping out, she slipped and fell. My arms shot out to her. I caught her around the waist, and out of reflex, she threw her arms around my neck. We were suddenly face to face. She took a deep breath as she ran her nose along my jawline causing goosebumps to sprout under my skin.

"Mmmm, you smell so good," she said as she continued to nuzzle into my neck. This contact was doing dangerous things to my self-control, and I stiffened to get ahold of myself. But I couldn't. I scooped her into my arms and took off toward the cabin. I had to get her to her room and lay her down as soon as possible. Liam was standing at the doorway, watching.

"I need Lexi," I said as I was taking the stairs two by two. Someone else needed to look after her because I didn't have the self-control to be alone with her.

We made it to the guest room where Henny was staying. I nudged the door open with my knee and walked her to the bed. When I went to lay her down, she did not release the hold on my neck, and we both went tumbling down in a heap on the king-size mattress. I tried to catch myself, but I managed to fall on top of her. I didn't move fast enough, and she coiled her legs around my waist. Grabbing my shirt, she pulled me even closer and was looking at me through sooty lashes. Her lips were a fraction from mine when I completely froze. I wanted her, but not like this.

"Stay with me," she whispered as she moved my cheek with her head and softly bit my ear, sucking my earlobe into her mouth. That was that, I was done. I felt my irises changing and knew it was a matter of seconds before the Alpha wolf would be taking over.

"Lexi!" I shouted.

I turned to look at the door, feeling both Lexi and Bran's appearance. Bran was sitting there, open mouth agape after the interaction he'd just witnessed.

"Get the fuck out of here!" I screamed and that seemed to pull him from his stupor. It was then that Henny pulled me close once more. The second that Lexi came into the room, I took off through the door. No sooner than I had made it to the basement, I shifted, surrendering myself to the wolf.

FIFTEEN

HENNY

I woke up the next morning, and my head pounded. I was hit with the sudden urge to vomit. *What the hell?* The feeling only intensified as I leaped from the bed, running to the bathroom to empty the little contents I had left in my stomach. Sitting on my heels after leaning over the toilet, I rubbed my hands over my forehead, trying to soothe the ache. Standing up, I brushed my teeth and splashed cold water on my face. That seemed to trigger the memories. The events of the following night flowed back to me in a hazy fashion. The entire scene at the club, the way my body moved, and remnants of a fight that broke out between Cole and Archer lingered in my mind. I remembered the way my body flushed with want when he announced to everyone that I was his. One of the strongest memories I had was making eye contact with Cole's green eyes, which displayed not only anger and aggression but also passionate hunger. The memory made my cheeks blush.

Images of leaving came next with Bran and Cole fighting in the parking lot, followed by the drive home and arriving back at the cabin. I couldn't get my footing, and that's when I remembered the way I wrapped my arms around his neck and became uncomfortably close in his personal space.

When we entered my room the night before, scenes of wrapping my legs around his waist and tumbling down to the bed came to mind, and I remembered that in that moment, I wanted nothing more than for him to want me. At first, I thought that he was trying to get away from me, but now I see that he was fighting an internal battle with himself. Not only was he trying to be the good guy, but I tried to throw myself at him the entire time. Thoughts came back into my mind on the way I touched him and then…*Oh my God*! I bit and sucked on his ear. My entire body flushed with embarrassment.

I also remember Lexi telling me about an elixir, and helping me through its effects. It felt like a bad drinking binge. Walking out of the bathroom into the bedroom, another wave of dizziness hit me, and I closed my eyes, trying to steady myself against the doorframe. Cole's deep, rich voice entered the room.

"Careful, it's still in your system. You're going to feel a little woozy."

My body tingled at the recognition of Cole's voice and electric energy buzzed between us. I hated the way he affected me. Never in my entire life did anything seem to unsettle me more than the man in front of me. I opened my eyes, my gaze meeting his.

"Are you okay?" he asked when I didn't respond.

Upon seeing him, the memory of me sucking his ear into my mouth created another rush of embarrassment, and I couldn't control the unbelievable word vomit that flowed out of my mouth next. "I'm sorry that I sucked you!" I blurted, both of us shocked by the words I spoke.

Cole's eyebrows shot up to his hairline, and his eyes grew wide at the statement.

"I mean, I'm sorry I sucked your. . .bit your. . . .." *Stop talking!* "I'm sorry that I was inappropriately close with you last night." I had to look away because I couldn't stand making eye contact with him anymore after the mortifying words I just said. Hearing him chuckle, I met his gaze once more and was greeted by the most dazzling smile I'd ever seen. He could have asked for anything in that moment, and I would have given it to him. He was beautiful.

"Ah yeah, that was quite the experience," he responded, nodding his head. My eyes went directly to his Adam's apple as he swallowed, trying to appease this seemingly awkward moment.

We stood there for a while, staring at each other, when he finally broke the spell. I felt like a complete dummy for drooling over him.

"We were able to find some information last night, and we can talk about it if you're ready. But if you need a few more minutes, let me know."

Perking up at the thought of there being some information on my family, I immediately jumped at the chance. We made our way down to the kitchen, and I wondered if anyone had been a witness to my embarrassment. My suspicion was immediately confirmed.

"Oh hey, Mike Tyson!" Bran shouted from across the room as Cole's entire family turned in my direction, causing my skin to turn a shade of crimson. Never had I been more embarrassed than I was in that moment. The rest of his family seemed to be enjoying the joke as they all suppressed smiles, most likely for my benefit. They thought it was funny? I chucked the first thing that I could find at Bran's head. Not expecting it, it knocked right into his beautiful face. Lucky for him, it was a squishy ball, not lucky for me, it didn't leave any impacting damage. Cassie howled with laughter, and even Liam was laughing. After a few minutes, we settled.

"Henny" Liam started. "I'm glad to see that you are feeling better. What happened last night was never our intention. If we thought for a second something like that was going to happen, we never would have gone." There was genuine empathy in his gaze, and he seemed sincere.

"I know," I replied. "I trust you guys."

Liam gave me an appreciative nod.

"I know you would never put me in jeopardy," I continued. "Thank you for what you did to keep me safe. Cole said that you found some information?"

Liam nodded. "It's not much, but it's something."

SIXTEEN

COLE

I sat and watched her from the doorway as Liam was explaining everything we learned about the vampires. I noticed Henny's body was tightening with anger at the situation. It took everything I had not to go over there and soothe the worry that was flooding her beautiful face. *Go to her.* The wolf side of me was whimpering, but I couldn't do it just yet, I still had to figure out how we were going to do this. How was I going to introduce the connection? There were a lot of obstacles that were standing in our way, but all I worried about was keeping her safe. Keeping what was *mine* safe. Not to mention, after all was said and done, what if she didn't feel the same way? My chest constricted at the thought.

While my family was plotting what to do next, I could visibly see the anger radiating from her. She needed to get it out, needed to release some of the emotion, or she was going to crack. She had the constant persona of being tough, but I saw right through it; mostly because I act the same way. Lexi seemed to notice Henny's body language as well.

"Henny, I know this is a lot to take in. Why don't you take some time to process everything? We can talk more about it later," she said.

Not making eye contact with anyone, Henny left the room. I went to follow her when Lexi stopped me.

"Give her some time," she said when she grabbed my forearm as I was walking out. I took a deep breath and nodded.

After we had finished up our plan and knew what we would do next, I went looking for Henny. It had been a few hours, and I had hoped the reprieve would have given her a little bit of time to cool off. I knew she hadn't gone far because I still felt her presence everywhere. Looking around the property, though, I couldn't find her. There was one final place to look. Always the warrior, she had somehow found her way down to our small training room. When I opened the door, she was working out her aggression on a punching bag. How she even found out about this place or found clothes to train in, I had no idea.

She had her back to me, but she stiffened when she felt my presence. Further entering the training room, I noticed how the tight workout clothes were clinging to her body. I followed the sweat that was slipping down the back of her neck and the way the shorts curved around her firm body. If my initial intention was not to fixate on her, I was failing, miserably. Strolling to her side, I leaned against the wall with my arms folded, staring at how aggressively she was taking out her frustration on the workout equipment. I understood how she felt. After the way she touched me last night, I was harboring a lot of frustrations of my own.

"Your form is off," I said flatly stopping her dead in her tracks. I was trying to help her, but the way she reacted, she took it as an insult.

"Excuse me?" she replied.

I tried to explain. "Your knuckles aren't tight enough. The flats of your fingers are going to hit first instead of your knuckles. You're angry. You don't fight as efficiently as you would when you aren't emotionally involved." This generated an unemotional laugh out of her.

"I've trained with some of the best trainers in the country while attending the most elite hunter academy in the United States, not to mention, I'm one of the best hunters in this province. I think my form is fine."

Yep, she definitely took my comment as an insult. She maintained her eye contact with the punching bag, not even looking in my direction. Frustrated, I was getting needy and required her attention.

"I said that your form was off when you were emotionally invested, not that you have bad form in general. Also, you're hitting a bag that can't hit you back." That made her look my way. I was feeling testy.

"I'm sorry. If you'd like, I can go grab a vampire and bring him back here so you can better guide my fighting skills? Would that work for you?" Her jaw was ticking and the more and more upset she got, the more and more I was feeling her frustration. My body was tensing up as well. Sometimes, werewolves are empathetic to how their mates were feeling. I must have been feeding off her anger. Not to mention I was already cranky; the sexual tension I was feeling was mounting, and after last night, it was at an all-time high.

"Listen, I get it. You're upset about your family but—"

"Upset? You think I'm upset? I'm furious!" *Punch.* "This is all my fault!" *Punch.* "I was supposed to protect them. I don't even know where they are, or if they're okay. And Gareth? Don't even get me started on Gareth because I'm going to rip out his throat the next time I see him." *Roundhouse kick.*

"See, this is exactly what I mean. You're pissed, so worried about it being your fault that you're not focusing on what you can do next to solve it. Instead of using your aggression to make you stronger, you're making yourself weak. You're wallowing." I was baiting her.

Instinct kicked in as she turned to take a swing in my direction, my forearm blocking her before she was able to make contact. Anger flared in her eyes that I blocked her punch and her other hand came around almost as fast. She threw her knee up, and I tried to block that, but my arm accidentally swiped the back of her knee causing her to lose balance, and her back slammed onto the floor, hard. I went tumbling with her. Her eyes winced momentarily, but she checked it immediately. Once I had her down, I moved my pelvis over her hips as I grabbed her flailing arms and put them over her head.

"Henny, will you just stop! I'm not the bad guy here, okay. I'm just trying to help. I have to know that you're okay, that you can take care of yourself. You don't get it. I have to protect you," I said furiously, my eyes never leaving hers.

"But that's the thing, Cole. You don't! You just met me, and this isn't your fight! Why do you even care so much?" she exclaimed as both of our breathing increased.

"Well, when you are someone's ma—" but I stopped myself. After everything that's happened, I still hadn't thought of how I was going to talk to her about the mate connection, and I hadn't had time to gauge how she'd react.

"When you're someone's what, Cole?" she said through gritted teeth. But I didn't respond, I couldn't yet.

God, didn't she get it? No matter what happened or what she did, I would follow her anywhere. That was it, the mate bond, there was no fighting it anymore. In those seconds, I realized that I would follow this girl to the ends of the earth, even if it meant going to Satan himself. As we stared at each other for a few seconds, I suddenly realized how very close our bodies were touching and how heavy both of us were breathing, anger radiating from within.

"Henny. . .," I started.

"Get off of me, Cole!" she shouted. I moved my hands off her wrists and slid off her body as she shot up and stormed out of the room. I fell back and sat with my hands on my knees, then flopped down on the mats with my hands over my face. That did not go how I wanted it to.

"Good job, bro," I heard Bran laugh as he yelled from the door.

Not having the energy to move and deal with him, I flipped him off while wondering how I was going to fix this.

SEVENTEEN

HENNY

Going back to my room, I was absolutely fuming. What the hell was Cole thinking? He tried to talk about how I fought? *He's only trying to help. All he has been doing is trying to help.* I took the tape off my wrists and threw it on the bed. At least I was able to get some training in. I was thankful for Lexi lending me the stuff.

I stood near the window, pouting, when there was a knock at the door. I knew it was Cole, so I didn't respond. I couldn't handle him right now. The door started to open, and I turned around to tell him exactly where he could go when Lexi and Cassie peeked their heads into the room.

"Hi Henny, we wanted to check on you. May we come in?" Lexi asked formally, whereas Cassie just barged in before I answered. She was a little brass, and I liked her more and more.

"We heard what our jerk brother did," Cassie remarked.

"Oh, he told you?" I questioned feeling a little aggravated that he would have tattled on me.

"No, we literally heard it," Cassie stated. "Werewolf hearing," she said twirling her finger into the air. *Well, that's embarrassing.*

"It's not uncommon," she continued. "Unfortunately, Cole is the king of tall, dark, and bratty. He has a chip on his shoulder most of the time. Don't take it personal, he doesn't like when people are better than him," Cassie said, and I suppressed a smile. "So! As a peace offering, Lexi and I have brought you something that will hopefully make you feel better. We know how hard these last few days have been for you."

"Okay, but there is one thing I need to know," I asked, and both the girls nodded. "I'm really gracious for all the help that your family has given me; how welcoming you guys are. But at the end of the day, I'm a hunter. Even though we are not natural enemies, our kind isn't exactly friends, either. Please don't think I'm not appreciative because I am, but you just met me. I'm causing a lot of trouble for you." That was just something I couldn't let go, it was in my nature. We were not ones to be so trusting. But these werewolves, they trusted so blindly and so passionately.

"It's complicated," Lexi answered.

"Are you going to elaborate?" I questioned, raising an eyebrow while leaning against the window sill.

Lexi looked at me and let out a long breath. "Anything that Cole does is always so calculated. He never acts out on anything unless it's for a specific measure. Sometimes we don't always know what that reason may be, or even agree with it, but that's what we do as a pack. We follow and trust our Alpha. There is a reason Cole saved you in the warehouse that night. He brought you back here to the pack for protection. He announced that under no circumstance was anything to happen to you. And that's it," she shrugged. "That's all we needed. You're ours to protect now. He hasn't openly said it because he is well, stubborn, but he trusts you, so we do, too."

I was completely blown away by her response as that was not the answer I expected. They loved so honestly and freely. Tears pricked my eyes as they accepted me so openly that it reminded me of my own family. I nodded my head and blinked the tears away.

"Thank you" I stated.

"You're welcome," Lexi answered with a soft smile.

"Okay!" Cassie jumped up, squealing and clapping. "Now for the surprise—wine!"

A few hours and a couple of bottles of wine later, we all laughed and learned about each other. The more wine we consumed, the more we laughed and the louder we became. It felt good to just relax. We didn't hear the door open.

"Sweet Jesus," Bran laughed, "It smells like a winery in here."

We all laughed as Bran came into the room. My eyes caught Cole's, and I immediately looked away, still mad at him for our interaction today.

"Hi, baby!" Lexi yelled as she launched herself at Liam, who was laughing too. Apparently, he found this comical. I think that's the most emotion I'd seen him have. "We just had a little," *hiccup.* "butt of wine," *hiccup.*

Did she just say butt of wine?

"I can see that," Liam said softly as he brushed his fingers down her cheek. Even though Lexi was severely intoxicated, he looked at her adoringly, and my heart tightened at the devotion.

"More like I can smell it," Bran replied as he scrunched his nose and looked into one of the many empty wine bottles that filtered in the room.

I laughed at Bran's comment, feeling a tingly heat radiate from the doorway. My eyes, once again, found Cole. Looking as delicious as ever, his broad form causally leaned against the doorframe, apparently unfazed by the scene around him. His eyes bored into mine.

"Okay, baby, let's get you to bed," Liam said as he tossed Lexi over his shoulder, and she squealed with delight. "He's taking me to beddddd!" she laughed as both of them walked out the door.

"Lightweight!" Cassie yelled. "There is still an entire bottle of Moscato here!"

"I can help with that," Bran replied in excitement as he came further into the room.

Leave it to Cole to turn the mood sour. "We're done drinking for the night," Cole commanded, never taking his eyes off mine.

I felt my body flush. Was he really telling me what to do? It irritated me.

"You guys can stay," I retorted defiantly, standing from my seat, but I stumbled into the loveseat right next to me. If it hadn't been there to catch my fall, I probably would have ended up my face.

"Leave," was all he said as he shot the command to his sister and brother.

Cole sauntered to me similar to the way a lion stalked its prey. Rooted to my spot by the intensity of his gaze, I couldn't take my eyes off of him.

"Okay, this is super awkward. Cassie, let's go drunk pants. I'm pretty sure Liam went shopping today. I believe we have snacks that will go perfectly with that bottle of Moscato you have there," Bran pulled the arm of his little sister, who stuck out her tongue like a petulant child as she walked out of the room.

"Later, Hen!" Cassie clamored as she blew an air kiss over to me.

I suppressed a giggle as she acted like she was casting a fishing pole to reel me in as Bran finally pulled her free of the rigid atmosphere that Cole left in his wake. They shut the door behind them.

Now that I was alone with Cole, the defiance and confidence that I showed wore off. To ease my nervous state, I looked everywhere except at him as my hand started to twirl the necklace around my neck.

"Are you done?" he asked cocking his head to the side. This was turning into my favorite gesture of his.

Cole slowly made his way toward me until he stood right in front of me. Instant fuzziness clouded my judgment, and I couldn't tell if it was from the alcohol or Cole's intimidating presence.

"So, what was the occasion that brought on all the drinking?" Cole whispered as he leaned into me and both of his hands landed on either side of the chair, boxing me in.

"You're a jerk," I replied, mad at how he made me feel. It was increasingly apparent that I couldn't control myself around him, and I didn't like it.

Cole tried to hide a smile at my comment. We were only inches apart, and I felt the heat coming from his skin. Oh my God, he smelled absolutely divine. Like pine forest after a fresh rain. I closed my eyes, and I leaned in a little closer.

"So why am I a jerk?" he asked, his voice so smooth it felt like it caressed my skin, causing my eyes to flutter back open. His eyes dropped from mine to my lips and then back up again.

"Well, for one, you don't play nice with others," I said.

"Oh, I think I play very well with others," he said huskily.

My breath hitched at the double meaning of his words. "Oh good, it's just me," I answered.

The things this man did to me on a normal day, let alone when wine coursed through my system, made me woozy with lust. For the second time, Cole was too much for me in an altered state.

"Listen," Cole said with a sensitive nature. "I wasn't trying to be a jerk today, it's just the way you came at me caught me off guard. I need to know that you can take care of yourself if, for any reason, I'm not around. I never meant to undermine you, Henny."

The striking green of his eyes was absolutely mesmerizing, and they rang with sincerity. It was at that moment, a thought crossed my mind. *You're falling for him.* I took a deep breath. I needed space. I couldn't handle how gorgeous he was. I couldn't think straight.

"Stop looking so, glexy," I said. *Wait, what?* "Oh!" I exclaimed as I brought the tips of my fingers to my mouth, covering the expression and trying to mask my embarrassment.

Cole started laughing, really laughing, as he flashed the most alluring smile.

I closed my eyes to memorize that beautiful sound. I also closed my eyes because I felt absolutely mortified. *Goddamned wine.* "I meant to say gorgeous, but I was thinking sexy, and it just came out wrong, I mean together." I really wished I would stop speaking. My attempt to regain my composure clearly wasn't working to my favor.

Cole reached up and brushed his thumb over my cheek. I froze in place due to the fierceness of his touch. I never wanted it to end.

"You think I'm gorgeous and sexy?" Cole whispered, our lips only inches apart.

Please kiss me, I thought.

Cole's hand moved off my cheek as he reached down and grabbed my fingers. His thumb was rubbing circles on the top of my hand. The gesture was surprisingly intimate. I moved to touch him but winced at the sudden pain in my back. I tried to hide the gesture, but he noticed. It felt as if ice water was thrown on the heated moment, and Cole straightened to attention.

"What's wrong?" he asked, concerned.

"Nothing," I responded and tried to move away from him, but the more I moved, the more my back hurt. The alcohol started to wear off and the after effects from this afternoon wore on my body. Concern marred Cole's face, and then anger met his features as he realized what was wrong.

"I hurt you today, didn't I?" he asked.

I tried shaking my head no, but he cut me off.

"Henny, did I hurt you?"

"It's nothing, really."

"Turn around and let me see," he asked.

"Cole, I'm fine, really, I—"

"Let me see," he flared.

Judging by the seriousness in Cole's voice, I didn't want to fight with him, so I turned around. He asked permission, and I felt his fingers lift up the back of my shirt. I heard the sharp intake of breath as he saw the bruise on my back. It probably didn't help that the after effects from Gareth on the night we met were still visible.

He slowly put my shirt back into place and grabbed my hips lightly so that my back was flush against his rock-hard chest. His lips were at my ear, and I instantly had goosebumps at his closeness.

"I'm so sorry I hurt you," he whispered. Leaning his forehead against the back of my head. I leaned into his touch, but he backed away. When I went to turn around to protest, he was already out the door, leaving me behind.

EIGHTEEN

COLE

I walked to the study of the cabin and went over to the cabinet where we kept the liquor. I grabbed the whiskey from the shelf and a glass and poured a shot, throwing it back to make room for another. *I fucking bruised her.* After seeing what I had done to Henny, my skin crawled. I was disgusted. The second shot came quickly after.

"Are you alright?" Liam said as he was standing in the doorway, and I turned around to face my older brother. Seeing the look of concern on his face reminded me of our father.

"This is a lot harder than I thought," I said. I'm not sure what made me want to tell him the truth, but I did it anyway.

"Well, it's not supposed to be easy, I'm not sure why you're fighting it so much," Liam responded as he casually pocketed his hands in his jeans.

"All of this would be a lot easier if you were Alpha. I'm not meant for this, I don't want it. You would have made better decisions," I said staring into my empty glass.

"Yeah, well my decisions might not have led you to her," he replied, and I looked up at him. He was right.

Liam stepped into the study, pouring me another drink and making one for himself. He swished it around in his glass for a second and then threw his back, too.

"Stop doubting yourself. It's not the Alpha mentality that you're doubting, it's your feelings for her. You're scared of how she's going to react once she finds out."

I walked over to the couch and sat down, leaning my elbows on my knees while running my thumb around the glass. I looked into the blazing fire of the fireplace. The rhythmic motion of the flames brought fourth my truest fear.

"She might leave," I spoke.

"She could stay," Liam answered, coming to sit beside me.

I faced my brother. "This wasn't how this was supposed to happen. This wasn't how it was supposed to work."

Liam laughed. "This isn't how anything is supposed to work," he responded. "You had a mate connection with a gorgeous, strong-willed woman who cares about what she believes in and fights even harder for it. Life sucks for you," he said jokingly as he smiled.

Liam rarely smiles, so I let that one slide. "I just keep thinking what Mom and Dad would say. Henny isn't like us, I'm not sure how they would have felt about it."

"Well, first of all, it appears that Henny will be able to keep your broody ass in check, so Dad would have loved that. And Mom would see her strengths, her passions, her loyalty. You and I both know it wouldn't matter what she is, Mom would love her all the same. Cole, you need to stop fighting your feelings for her and just accept fate."

My brother was staring at me now like he wanted me to accept what he was saying with the snap of his fingers. Finding our mates was something that we always knew would happen, someone we had always hoped to find. Henny might as well live in a different world than me, our lives were so different. I'm not sure how she would feel about this, not sure how she would feel about being bound to someone. She wasn't exactly someone you could claim.

"I'm not sure it's that easy," I said as I threw another shot back. I sat back on the couch taking a deep breath as if the room in front of me would provide all of life's answers.

"Then make it that easy," he responded. He slapped my back and started to walk out the door when his phone pinged. "Looks like we found the nest you were looking for, we should probably hit it while the tip is fresh if we want to find anything out."

"We'll go tomorrow," I replied.

Liam nodded and walked out the door.

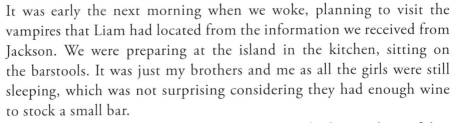

It was early the next morning when we woke, planning to visit the vampires that Liam had located from the information we received from Jackson. We were preparing at the island in the kitchen, sitting on the barstools. It was just my brothers and me as all the girls were still sleeping, which was not surprising considering they had enough wine to stock a small bar.

Henny was the first to walk in and meet us, looking as beautiful as ever, like she hadn't spent the entire previous night drinking her weight in alcohol. Her eyes met mine, and a blush tinted her cheeks as she mumbled good morning. Liam had offered her some coffee, which she graciously accepted. She finally spoke to us.

"What's going on? You guys look like you're discussing something important," she inquired.

She's as observant as always. Liam was the one to reply.

"We got a tip of a vampire cell that sounded like the same vampire Jackson's pack found. We're thinking that it might have something to do with Gareth. Surprisingly, it's just outside of downtown New Orleans."

"Great, when are we leaving?" Henny asked as she sipped her coffee.

"You are not going," I said.

Her head snapped up, and she took a breath to argue, but I beat her to it.

"Need I remind you what happened at the club?"

"That wasn't my fault," Henny said through grated teeth.

"And I understand that, but it's not worth something happening to you again. I won't risk you."

Bran cocked an eyebrow at the bold declaration as Liam's words from last night rang in my ears. Something that drastic was the only way to get Henny's attention.

"Not to mention," I continued. "That was just going to see another pack of werewolves, this is literally walking into a vampire lair. What if Gareth is there?" I asked.

"All the more reason I need to go!" Henny replied, anger apparent in her features. She was getting more irritable, but the veracity of her personality was only making her more attractive.

I suppressed a smile because she was having the complete opposite effect on me than what she was intending to.

"Ah, yeah, that's not happening, I will lock you in a closet if I have to," I said as I took a sip of my coffee, my eyes locking with hers. I met her gaze, challenging her to defy me. I stood up, so my body language reached the extent of the authority I wanted it to, and I was answered with silence. The only thing she did was push off the counter she was leaning against and stormed out of the room.

I turned around, and both of my brothers had smiles on their faces.

"What?" I spat, annoyed with their reactions.

"Well, that went well," Bran said.

"Also, just wondering if you guys can go ahead and have sex already to ease the sexual tension in here. It's nauseating," Liam replied.

Bran's mouth dropped open as Liam was never one to make outlandish comments like that, and we were all laughing because it was so unexpected. After the laughter died down, we got back to planning what we were going to do for that night.

Surprisingly, we were able to leave with just the three of us. I was expecting Henny to come crashing through the door, demanding to come; however, I hadn't heard a single thing from her the rest of the day. She was pissed. I would deal with it tomorrow. At least I knew she'd be safe.

One thing was for sure, I was glad that Henny had listened because this place was as sketchy as fuck. The ultimate vampire hideaway. We parked further down the road and walked the rest of the way on foot so we could be as quiet as possible. Vampires didn't have as advanced hearing as werewolves, but we still didn't want to make a scene. Right before we entered the building, we went over the plan one more time, discussing the different ways to get out, in case this went bad. We were going to go in, look around to see if we could find anything on Jonah, and then leave. I took the north entrance, and Bran and Liam both went in through the south side of the building.

As I stepped into the building, I was suddenly hit with a sense of déjà vu, remembering the night I rescued Henny. It had the same creepy feel to it. Taking a few more steps in, I was becoming more and more uneasy. The werewolves had a less than stellar relationship with hunters, but it was civil. But with vampires, we hated each other just for sport. We needed to take extra precautions.

My senses were heightened as I made my way down a darkened hallway. It seemed like more and more darkness was coating the building, and I cursed at myself for even coming. I should have known better, and my senses were screaming at me that this was a bad idea. I pulled out my phone to text my brothers that we needed to get out. No service was listed on my screen. *Of course.* At least I hadn't heard any type of movement. Maybe they had moved on?

I made my way downstairs, and my wolf senses were screaming at me. I detected movement from the balcony I had just left. I glanced up and saw nothing, but when I turned back around, I noticed them. No less than five vampires were currently in the vicinity of where I was standing, essentially boxing me in.

"So glad you could join us, Mr. Martin," the vampire master announced.

He couldn't have been more than a year or two older than I was. He was dressed in what looked like an expensive designer suit and had a clean-shaven face. His blond hair was gelled and slicked back. His height matched mine. I probably would have been able to take him, but with four other vampires, that was going to be a problem. This was the man in charge; his air of superiority told me as much.

"What do you want?" I asked, trying to buy myself some time until my brothers were able to find me.

He was making his way closer to where I was standing, and from what I could see out of my peripheral vision, the other vampires were closing in as well.

"What I want is you out of the way. You've become an annoying problem that I was sent to deal with," he replied as if he was bored.

I stood even taller, crossing my arms. "Listen, buddy, I think that you're mistaken—"

"No, I'm not," he said with a sinister smile, and then he snapped his fingers. Before I could make my move or begin to shift, a sharp pain went shooting through my back, and I dropped to my knees, grabbing the pain. I knew what it was the moment it touched my skin. *Silver.* The shot itself wasn't fatal, but the silver surrounding the bullet would be lethal. The pain was unlike anything I have ever felt. Liam and Bran would definitely sense their Alpha's distress. Gasping for air, I was struggling to breathe.

"Why are you doing this?" I asked as strongly as I could.

"Well Mr. Martin," he replied. "Your services of protecting Henrietta Bradford are no longer needed. Think of it as a better purpose for our future, think of the greater good," he said as casually as if he were discussing the weather. My heart rate spiked as the pain amplified.

"What is that supposed to mean?" I coughed as blood littered the ground in front of me.

"Don't you worry, you will soon find out," he replied.

"If you touch her, I swear I'll rip your fucking throat out," I forced out, coughs racking my chest. I prayed that Bran and Liam were alright.

"You see, judging by your current state, I don't think you will," he said as he turned around to the other vampires who were now gathered in front of me.

"Complete the wolfsbane circle so the others can't get to him and then end him. We need to move, I can't imagine that Miss Bradford is too far from here. She is to be delivered to Mr. Frederickson alive."

Wolfsbane? Fuck. This wasn't going to end well, and I prayed that my brothers made it out alive because someone needed to look after Henny after all of this went down.

As the master started to walk away, the remaining vampires encircled me. I tried my hardest to shift, but the severity of my injury was preventing me from doing it. One vampire drew the weapon which had initially tagged me. As the poison from the silver was creeping into my body, I realized this quite possibly was the last night of my life. Thoughts of my family flew through my head. Liam, Bran, Lexi, Cassie. . .but what filtered through my mind the most was Henny. The first time that she had smiled at me, the night I held her close after her nightmare, more and more images flashed in my mind from a future we would never have. Our first kiss, our first time, the night she would receive my mark. Images of her hair swaying in the wind, laughing as she was chasing a child with chocolate hair while another was growing in her belly. The only comfort I had was knowing that her face would be the last thing I would see.

As I was accepting my fate, a shotgun was pointed directly at my face, holding what I was sure were silver bullets. As I closed my eyes, thinking of her face once more, a dark shadow descended from the balcony to land right in front of me. It was an avenging angel. No, it was *my* avenging angel.

NINETEEN

HENNY

I jumped off the balcony, landing directly in front of Cole. My heart thundered in my chest, worried that I wasn't going to get to him in time. It didn't take long to figure out that he wasn't going to let me go, so I dropped it, acting like I had stayed behind. I followed them the second they left.

"Gentleman," I announced. "Having a party and I wasn't invited?" I asked with cool indifference. "How incredibly rude." I feigned annoyance while taking in all of the vampires who encircled us. One in particular turned around, his eyes glittering with delight.

"Henny, what the fuck are you doing, get out of here," Cole said again as he coughed up more blood.

Rage rippled through me. I was going to end each and every single asshole in this room. First to go would be the vampire who shot him.

"I don't see how you are going to make it out of this one Miss Bradford," the vampire master said.

"I'm assuming Gareth sends his regards?" I asked, stalling as I gauged how I would take them all out.

"I don't think this could have played out any easier than what he planned; he will be thrilled," he responded, clasping his hands together. The master thought he won, but he had another thing coming.

"Well then," I took a step forward. "You can tell him to go to hell. Actually, maybe write a memo, because you all will be dead."

Anger flared in his eyes at my comment.

I turned to Cole, and his pale face wore a mask of open fear. "I will not let them take you from me," I replied as I stared straight into his eyes. I didn't give him time to answer as I turned back around. I drew my two blades, and the force of courage that came over me was empowering. One thing was for certain, they were not going to touch what was mine. I took a defiant step forward.

"Alright, who's first?" I asked.

"Henny, No!" Cole cried from behind me, barely sounding conscious. That's when the first two vampires lunged at me.

I saw them coming and charged at them. They were fast, but I was faster. With one swipe of the blade with my right hand, the vampire on that side never had a chance. His head rolled off his shoulders, and his body dropped to the ground within seconds. I caught the second vampire in the stomach with my blade as I whirled around, slicing my second blade into his chest. He was probably still alive, but this bought me some time.

"Kill the werewolf!" I heard the master yell, and that's when I noticed the third vampire making his way to Cole.

With a force I didn't even know I had, I grabbed him around the waist, tackling him forward as we both crashed to the ground. Rolling so that I was on top of him, I pulled the small wooden crossbow that was tucked into the back of my pants and shot it right through the heart of the vampire beneath me. *Two down.*

I looked over to an unconscious Cole and went to him when a searing pain shocked my throat. The fourth vampire sank his teeth into my neck, rendering a pain unlike anything I have ever felt before. I felt him rip the flesh from my body as he tried to wrap his arms around me.

I pulled an additional blade from my boot and stabbed him straight through the torso. This caused him to fall forward, and as he collapsed, he bit me a second time on the side, which caused the pain to worsen. I turned around, kicking him in the chest, hurtling him backward. I scrambled toward Cole, making sure they wouldn't go near him.

The three remaining vampires descended on me, backing me into a corner. My heels backed into Cole's unconscious form.

"I said she is to be kept alive! Now get her, and let's go," the master yelled.

My attention momentarily snapped to the two massive, growling wolves that were stuck outside of the barrier of wolfsbane and pigments of silver. *Bran and Liam.* They looked more like rabid dogs than anything from the aggression in their eyes. What once were brown eyes now glowed yellow. They would do anything to get in, do anything to save their Alpha.

The two wolves, although scary as hell, were more beautiful than anything I'd ever seen. The dominance and grace that both of them possessed was frightening but alluring. If the werewolves were to penetrate the barrier, the vampires would be in trouble.

The vampires closed in as my mind raced for options, but the situation was looking grim. I needed to do something drastic; I needed to do whatever it took to get Cole out of here safely. I took a breath to steady my thoughts. What I had in me was something I thought I would keep forever hidden; however, the time had come.

I had a secret. Daxon and I both did. My mind flashed to a memory of Daxon and me as kids. Our father sat us down and made us promise that we would never let anyone know what we could do, the full extent of our abilities.

"No one can know because of the prophecy, they won't understand its significance," my father said as Daxon and I both nodded in understanding.

It was imperative to keep our abilities a secret because it would make us targets, make us the hunted instead of the hunters. But in this moment, I would reveal my secret, I would do anything to save the man that I loved. *Loved.* That's when all hell broke loose.

I had summoned the power that I had buried so far down inside me, I thought it would never see the light of day. I felt the fever flood through my entire body as the heat of a blazing sun came forward, responding to my demand. I called the flames to my hands, and within seconds, my fingers were consumed with fire.

I took in the stunned and terrified looks of the three awestruck vampires. Snapping my fingers and flicking my wrist, a stream of fire shot toward the vampire who had bitten me. His body was engulfed in flames. His screams followed, and within a few moments, his body was ash. I turned back to the other two vampires, and their eyes were filled with fear. The fear they felt, brought on by my current state, must have warned of danger because as they turned to run, they ran in the direction of Bran and Liam. As if sensing their predicament, they stopped up short, one vampire faced me as the other turned to the two frenzied wolves.

"Ah, my darling, it appears you have a little secret," the master said, trying to hide the fear in his voice.

"Yes," I answered, my voice completely flat and void of emotion. "And now this secret is going to take you straight to hell."

I brought forth the fire once more and felt the power recharge. While the power generated, I also felt my strength slipping. From the sudden use of magic, the exhaustion grappled me at an alarming rate. Paired with the blood loss from the vampire bites on my neck and side, I was losing strength, fast. I needed to end this now.

I took both of my hands and shot two waves of fire at the remaining vampires. The whites of their eyes were the last thing that I saw before both of their bodies erupted into flames. As with the first vampire, the two remaining ones were reduced to dust in a matter of seconds. I felt consciousness slipping from my senses.

When the vampires were eliminated, I dropped to my hands and knees, trying to stay awake, needing to get Cole to safety. A howl brought me back as my head snapped to Liam and Bran. I used the only remaining remnants of magic that I had to generate a gust of wind to break the circle of wolfsbane and silver. That was the last bit of energy I had, and I dropped to the floor. With my blurred vision, I watched Bran and Liam, in their human form, race toward us. They were the last thing I remembered before I succumbed to darkness.

As consciousness came back to me, I felt comfortable, too comfortable. *Um, did I die?* I was almost in a state of comfortable bliss, that was, until I moved. I shifted in a different direction, and I felt like I had been hit by a bus. My body had hurt all over, and my head pounded. Not to mention the burning sensation from two very raw vampire bites.

I opened my eyes, and I shot up, despite the agony I experienced. Two firm hands steadied me.

"It's okay, you're alright," I looked up and met Liam's soft brown eyes, which were filled with concern. I was so thankful it was him. But upon realizing it was Liam, I noticed someone else was not in the room. A sense of dread washed over me.

"Oh God, Cole," I stated urgently.

"He's going to be okay. He's still unconscious, but thanks to you, he's alive," Liam responded.

I couldn't help the tears that stung my eyes as they fell freely from the relief that Cole was okay. I didn't care. As I cried, Liam enveloped me into a somewhat awkward hug, but I was soothed by his presence. What felt like a few minutes later, I pulled away and noticed his soaked shirt. I wiped the remaining tears off my cheeks.

"It appears you haven't been completely honest with us," he stated.

It wasn't accusatory or angry, more of just a general rhetorical statement.

I sighed. "It's complicated," I responded biting the inside of my cheek.

Liam sat softly on the side of the bed next to me. "I've got time."

TWENTY

COLE

Life is a funny thing. You take things for granted until you realize they were almost taken away. Even the small things; a first look, a first touch, a first kiss. In your mind, they were not a big deal until you're faced with never having them again.

In what I thought were the last moments of my life, all I could think about was not having kissed Henny. Never experiencing the feel of her lips on mine, how soft they were, the taste of her skin. Never wrapping my fingers through her hair as I pulled her lips closer to mine. I promised myself at that moment, if I made it out of there, I would never take for granted things that had not happened yet ever again.

More thoughts filtered into my mind while it dawned on me that she wasn't in the room. My last memory was of her descending from the balcony above me and dropping in front of me. That's where things had gotten fuzzy. I remembered her declaration saying she would not let them take me away from her. My heart was swelling at the proclamation. I woke with a start when I heard Bran beside me.

"Woah, Cole, easy. I need you to take it easy," Bran said holding his hands out to steady me.

"Where is Henny?" I said huskily, trying to clear my thoughts.

"She's fine, she's with Lexi now," he continued.

I threw my legs over the side of the bed. Even though Bran said the words, I needed to see for myself that she was okay. I shot out of bed, much to the dismay of my injury, which was screaming back. I charged next door to Henny's room, and I didn't even bother to knock as I bounded in.

Upon my entry, Henny was sitting on the bed, shirtless, wearing only a bra. This would have done dangerous things to me if it weren't for the fact that she had two enormous vampire bites on the right side of her body, one on her neck and the other on her torso. It sent me into a murderous rage. If it weren't for the look of shock on Henny and Lexi's faces, I would have lost it. Upon noticing my presence, Lexi gave Henny one of my thermal shirts. The thought of Henny wearing my clothing sent me into overdrive. Lexi turned back to her.

"You're going to be fine. I just want to keep an eye on those to make sure they heal correctly," Lexi said.

"Lexi, I need to speak with Henny privately," I said, never taking my eyes off of her.

Lexi smiled sweetly at Henny as she turned to walk out of the room. She kissed me on the cheek as she passed.

"I'm so glad that you're okay. You had us worried there for a minute," Lexi said as she exited.

Henny's eyes were relieved that I was standing in front of her.

"Are you okay?" we both said at the same time and then smiled at each other's reaction. I walked over to where she was sitting on the bed and stood directly in front of her. As Henny went to pull the shirt over her shoulders, I interjected.

"Stop," I said. "I need to see what they did to you."

"Cole," she said while shaking her head.

"I need to see what those mother fuckers did to you," I said through gritted teeth.

The seriousness of my tone must have convinced her because she stopped fighting me. Meeting my eyes directly, she brought the shirt back down and rested it in her lap, her eye contact had never broken mine. When she let the shirt fall to the bed, I almost lost my shit.

Henny had two half-moon bites on the right side of her body that were turning a nasty shade of red and already scabbing, which meant they were healing. As long as a vampire wasn't latched on to your skin for a long time, they didn't cause permanent damage. I gently ran my hand down the side of her neck and her ribs where the two bites were located on her body. It didn't go unnoticed how she jumped at my touch, or how it was causing a trail of goosebumps to erect in their wake. I was so mad at her for putting herself in harm's way for me. I dropped down to my knees in front of her, grabbing her face in my hands.

"God, Henny, what the fuck were you thinking, going after them like that? You could have died," I said choked up.

She closed her eyes, leaning into my palm. "I'd do it again if it meant nothing would happen to you, if it meant that you'd stay alive," she said as she opened her eyes back up to meet mine. Her penetrating gaze held so many emotions that it was hard to distinguish them all. After last night, something had changed between us. The electric energy that encircled our presence burned more vehemently as if the connection was recognizing what Henny was finally starting to understand. We were drawn to each other. But with these newfound emotions, traces of panic remained from the fact that she was almost taken away from me.

"My God, it was so fucking stupid, if something like that ever happens again, I need you to promise me—"

She cut me off. "Cole Martin," she whispered. "It will be you every time, you got that?" Henny answered with conviction.

Hope soared through me as I realized that she may have feelings for me. The thought of being mates now seemed possible. I realized what I was fighting all along. It only took a few days, but I was completely and undeniably in love with this girl. I moved even closer to her. We were now chest to chest, nose to nose. I gently lifted my shirt back over her head, and I rested my forehead against hers, trying to calm the racing heart her words had caused. It appeared to have that same effect on her. Our gazes met, and it was now my turn to lean into her touch as her palm caressed my cheek. Her fingers were soft on my skin as she rubbed the pad of her thumb over my bottom lip.

"What are we doing?" she whispered.

It was a general question, but it meant so much more. What were we doing with us? Our lips were a fraction apart when a knock at the door interrupted us. I turned to find Liam standing in the doorway. Henny's hands dropped from my face.

"I'm sorry, but Landon, Kay, and the rest of the Atlanta pack are here. They heard what happened to you and came right away. Landon wanted to speak with you but," he paused taking in the position that Henny and I were in. "I can tell him that you're not ready."

It was Henny who answered him. "No, it's okay. You should see them. They are concerned and came all the way from Atlanta. You should go talk to them," she said softly.

But I didn't want to be with them, I wanted to be with her. I nodded my head. "Okay. Will you come with me?" I asked her as Henny tried to hide the glint of satisfaction. I offered her my hand to help her stand up, but I paused leaning into her ear.

"This isn't finished," I said as I brushed the hair from her forehead.

She smiled and bit her lip. "I know," she responded as we walked out of the room.

TWENTY-ONE

HENNY

As we made our way down to the living room, I felt a lot of different emotions. I was so glad that Cole was okay, but our discussion was leading us somewhere I wasn't certain we could go. We were still hand-in-hand when we walked into the living area where a new group of individuals stood. Everyone ceased talking upon Cole's arrival. Landon and a woman briefly saw our arms connected before Cole let go to shake Landon's hand. Bran had a goofy grin, and his gaze met mine when he noticed Cole holding my hand. He waggled his eyebrows up and down. What a schoolgirl.

"Cole, we're so glad you're alright. We came down as soon as we heard," Landon declared.

"Thanks, man, I appreciate you guys coming down here. It appears we have a much bigger issue than we had originally thought," Cole responded.

While walking downstairs, Cole informed me that Landon's pack and he were lifelong friends. They all used to live in New Orleans; however, Landon's family had gone to Atlanta to try and establish their own pack. While Cole said that it hurt his father a little as the current Alpha, he respected their decision, and they remained close friends. Landon lost his parents also, so they had that connection.

"Well, that's what happens when you fraternize with hunters, things always get rigid," the female responded. *Um, what?*

"Excuse me?" I responded, but she bluntly ignored me.

Bran seemed to notice my opposition, so he stepped closer to me. Liam did the same on my other side.

The brunette walked over to Cole and gave him a seductive hug. When she pulled away, she kept her hands on his biceps and batted her gorgeously long eyelashes at him.

"I really don't know what we would have done if something would have happened to you," she cooed then kissed his cheek before backing away still holding his hand.

What. The. Fuck? Fury mounted inside me.

Cole stiffened as his eyes met mine. I couldn't control the amount of rage that flowed through my body at the thought of her touching him. It was very apparent that there was something going on between them at the way they intimately touched. Not to mention she was a supermodel, which didn't soften the blow. How could he not want someone who looked like that?

The brunette was probably around five foot nine with legs for days. Her long and perfectly straight chestnut hair cascaded down her back and chest, and she had a smile that would make even Liam drool. *Kay King.* I remember Cole saying her name as he told me about Landon. Never in my life had I felt self-conscious about my body until this moment.

"Uh, thanks, Kay. I appreciate you guys being here," Cole responded, his eyes coming back to mine.

"I know," she purred. "We have no problem helping you clean up someone else's mess," Kay finished as she directed her gaze to me.

Oh, she going to get it. "Listen, I'm not sure what your problem is here—" but she cut me off.

"You're the problem here," she said as she took a step toward me.

What little bit of sanity I had left was getting ready to go flying out the window.

"Kay, knock it off," Landon warned as he stepped closer.

"Actually," I met her step. "Your attitude seems to be the problem, and I'd be happy to adjust it for you," I seethed.

"Bitch, I'd like to see you try," she smiled defiantly at me.

I could tell blood rapidly pumped through my veins because the bite on my neck and ribs throbbed from the adrenaline coursing through my body.

"I'd ruin you," I said through gritted teeth, which only made her smile more.

"I'm not sure that you would because it looks like a vampire almost ruined you," she smiled placing a hand on her hip.

Three things happened at that moment; I snapped, she laughed, and I lunged. Faster than I thought I could have moved with my injuries, my fist connected with her face, striking her perfectly tanned nose. It probably wasn't the most honorable thing to do, but I wasn't thinking clearly at the moment.

They were all shocked at what happened, and six very large male werewolves stood, mouths agape, rooted in their spot as I continued my assault on Kay while she set loose a string of profanities. They all reacted at the same time because within seconds, two incredibly strong arms wrapped around my waist, pulling me away from her at the same time Landon pulled Kay in the other direction. The little bit of blood trickling down her nose gave me a tiny bit of satisfaction. But, it was Cole who pulled me off, and he was pissed.

"Henny, go to the study. I will be there in a second," he barked.

"If you think for one second—"

"Goddamn it, I said go!" he yelled.

I turned around to leave the room and headed up the stairs. Anger radiated through my system in disbelief that Cole had just dismissed me like that. What was I thinking? That Cole would defend me? Come with me? He was a werewolf, I should have known that he would defend and side with his own kind. It also stung that he sent me away so easily after the intimate moment we had just shared upstairs.

Once I made it into the study, I slammed the door behind me, noticing the pain emanating from my injuries. I endured so many emotions with everything that had happened over the last few days. I was dangerously close to my breaking point.

I sat in the chair, arms crossed as I bounced my knee. The door opened, and Cole sauntered in. I stood, and for a moment, we just watched one another. He closed the door behind him, and he turned back in my direction. I stood straighter to project my anger in Cole's direction. He broke the silence first.

"You broke her nose," he said flatly as he crossed his arms over his chest.

"Yeah, well she had it coming," I shrugged my shoulders.

"So, you punched her?" he questioned.

I was too angry to try and play nice. "I didn't do anything," I yelled back. I needed a distraction, or I was going to lose it again. I started to straighten the books that were on the shelves as I took deep, calming breaths.

"Listen, I know Kay seems rough around the edges," Cole started.

"That's an understatement," I chuckled, still facing the bookshelf.

"But she's loyal to my family," he replied.

Don't fucking care. "Yeah, well I guess you would know," I said turning back to him. I finally decided to make eye contact with Cole. I wanted to see his reaction.

"What's that supposed to mean?" he responded, glaring at me.

"Nothing, I just mean of course you would defend your *girlfriend*," I replied.

"She is not my girlfriend, nor has she ever been my girlfriend," he replied annoyed.

I chuckled, how rich. "Well, you could have fooled me," I said, but I had to look away from the intensity of his gaze. I turned back to the bookshelf like a coward. *Shit.* I looked over my shoulder as I saw Cole strolling toward me. I turned back around, trying to appear confident when he stopped right in front of me. I paced a few steps so my back was now against the shelf.

Placing his hands on either side of my head, he smiled. "You're jealous of Kay," he said.

Bingo. I lied. "I am not jealous of Kay," I said, only my body betrayed my voice because it sounded like I was on the verge of hyperventilating.

"You have no reason to be jealous," he purred, his body pushing into mine. Our faces were only centimeters apart.

"I am not jealous," I ground out.

Cole's gaze dropped from my eyes to my lips, and my body flushed all over. My heart pumped hard and fast, I thought it would come out of my chest. He moved his palm to my cheek, and I felt his hand shake. I had the same effect on him that he did on me.

"Good, because she isn't the one that I want," Cole whispered as his lips lightly brushed against mine not once, but twice, causing my heart to stop. He pulled away to gauge my reaction, to make sure it was okay, but we both knew it was okay, and we both reacted.

His lips crashed into mine.

TWENTY-TWO

COLE

Once Henny's lips were on mine, it seemed as if I had finally come up for air after being trapped underwater. Everything had been mounting to this point, the mate connection, the night of the club, almost losing each other. Kissing her for the first time felt better than I could have ever dreamed. The taste of her tongue and lips was something I could lose myself in for days. Like an addict, I had finally found my fix.

Grabbing her beautiful hips, I hoisted her up, and she wrapped her perfectly sculpted legs around my waist while I had pushed her even further into the wall. A soft moan escaped her mouth, and it encouraged me further. Matching my intensity, she opened to me, and I felt her tongue slip into my mouth running over my bottom lip. I growled with want, which only tempted her more as she took my bottom lip and sucked it into her mouth. As we kissed, her hands ended up tangled in my hair, and she pulled the strands on the nape of my neck gently.

"Table," she whispered.

I knew what she wanted. With her legs still wrapped around me, I carried her over to the table, placing her on the edge as she pulled me back to her. I didn't give a fuck about whatever was on the desk and pushed it off the side as I scooted her back. Her fingers started working the buttons on my shirt. I tore my lips away from hers, trailing kisses behind her ear, down her neck, onto her sternum, careful to avoid the injuries that were on her body. She threw her head back letting out a soft cry as my lips made their way back up to her collarbone.

Once she finished unbuttoning my shirt, it fell to a heap on the floor. My mouth had only broken contact with hers to slip the shirt over her head, and I threw it on the floor to join mine.

Resting her forehead against mine, I took in her nearly naked form. She was so goddamned gorgeous. Her bronze skin was smooth, and her breasts were the perfect size. Her stomach was flat from years of hard training. The only thing to mar her beautiful skin were the two vampire bites from when she saved me. Knowing she did that only made her more beautiful.

I flinched as her fingers touched the injury from the silver I had taken and worry crossed her face. But we healed quickly, it would probably be gone by morning.

"Hey," I said as I grabbed her chin. "It's okay," I confirmed.

She let out a shaky breath. "If I hadn't saved you, I don't know what I would have done," she said as she looked away from me, but I turned her face again so her eyes were directly on mine. Tears were floating in them.

I took her lips in mine again. Whereas before our kiss was hot and heavy, now our kiss was more intimate and passionate. Expressing what each of us didn't have to say, that in just a short while, we cared about each other. She pulled away once more as she ran her fingers down my Alpha mark, sending shivers through my body.

"You'll have to explain that," she whispered against my lips, and I smiled.

I met her lips once again.

138

The door to the study quickly swung open. "Cole, can you believe that Henny punched Kay—" Bran said as he came bounding into the room.

I quickly shifted Henny so Bran couldn't see her topless form and looked over my shoulder as his eyes widened at my naked back.

"Shit, I um, I'm sorry, ah, so very sorry," Bran replied as he shut the door as quickly as he opened it.

Bran's sudden appearance had caused our private and intimate moment to evaporate. I looked over at Henny with her eyes wide at having just been caught.

"Oh God," she said. "Oh God, I'm so sorry," she replied. Pushing me back, she slipped off the table and quickly grabbed her shirt and threw it over her head. "Henny, wait," I said as I called after her to calm her nerves, but she was already out the door, leaving me breathless again.

TWENTY-THREE

HENNY

I didn't know where I was going, but I knew I needed to get out of here. I needed time to think. My life had been flipped upside down in a matter of days, and it felt like life was crashing around me. Worried that if I went back to my room that Cole would follow; I went to the only other place that I knew outside the cabin—the lake. In the matter of a week, I saved Cole's life, been attacked by vampires, gotten in a fight with a werewolf, and kissed the most attractive guy I'd ever seen. Thoughts of Daxon and my dad flooded back to me.

And that's when I collapsed from the guilt. All this happened, and I hadn't once thought about Dax and Dad. My main reasoning behind all of this was to make sure they were okay; however, I had been so occupied with other events, I hadn't thought of even one way to help them. Out of all the emotions I felt in the last few days, guilt was the most overwhelming sensation. I dropped to my knees trying to catch my breath from it.

"Don't do that," I heard from in front of me. I lifted my head to find Liam standing there. "I can sense your guilt all the way from here."

I lifted an eyebrow in question, but he just shrugged. "It's a werewolf thing."

"I've done nothing to help them."

He didn't need further explanation, he knew what I was talking about. I sat back on my knees and blinked back the burning in my eyes. I wasn't going to lose it in front of Liam, not again.

"I've been so preoccupied with other things."

Liam came and stood in front of me, kneeling with his hands resting on his knees. "For fuck's sake, Henny, think of what you have been through. One of your most trusted friends betrayed you, your dad and brother are missing, you're completely on the run because you don't know who to trust, you were attacked by and then killed a group of vampires using whatever God knows for help, you saved my brother, and dealt with the wrath of Kay King. That's enough to make anyone crack. But you survived and broke a girl's nose," he said.

I suppressed a smile. I was really starting to like Liam, too. "But that's it. All of those things made me lose sight of the main issue here, Liam. My family is missing, and I was too worried about—" I brought myself up short.

Liam raised his eyebrows as if waiting for me to continue. When I didn't, he let out a sigh.

"My brother cares about you," he said.

I chuckled. "Your brother barely knows me," I replied. It was true, but that didn't mean I wanted it to be true.

It was Liam's turn to chuckle. "As if fate lets us control who we want?" Liam said, and then stopped himself from speaking further.

My eyes snapped to attention at his statement, and my breathing hitched, understanding the implication of what he just said. When werewolves meet their mates, it's instant. It doesn't matter who or where you are. The mate connection takes control, and they have no influence over it. *Holy shit.*

"I would have done the same thing," Lexi said as she joined Liam's side. Liam looked at her adoringly and smiled. "Kay is an absolutely horrendous person," she responded.

"I wouldn't have expected anything else, baby," Liam stood up and gave her the softest kiss on the lips. I had to look away at the intimacy.

"I just came out here to tell you that your brother is gone. It would probably be a good idea for you to stop by the apartment," Lexi said as she and Liam looked at me. I blushed.

"Okay, baby, can you take it from here?"

"Of course," Lexi answered. "Come on, Henny, I think I have some wine." I smiled and relaxed a little, following Lexi back to the cabin.

TWENTY-FOUR

COLE

I don't even know how I got there, but the next thing I knew my truck was pulling into the lot of my studio apartment. Even though I spend most of my time at the cabin, sometimes I just need space to myself. Thankfully, my parents had made some smart financial choices that left my family and me extremely comfortable. Not to mention, Liam taking over the family business kept a steady income for us all.

Coming to the apartment gave me time to determine what I was going to do next. After tonight, I knew I couldn't fight my feelings for Henny anymore, and I needed to tell her about the mate connection. I needed to figure out what I was going to say to convince her that this would work.

After a few drinks, I heard the front door to my apartment unlock and in walked Liam and Bran. As I was sitting on the couch, Liam poured Bran and himself a drink and then sat at the table across from me. My brothers both were looking at me expectantly.

"How can I make this work?" I asked. "I'm afraid it will scare her away," I announced.

"Well when a man and a woman love each other very much," Bran started, and I threw a pillow at his head.

"Well, if Jonah is the type of leader we think he is, the hunters have full knowledge of every aspect of our species. She knows this happens. They take mates themselves, she has to know how this feels. Trust in her, trust the connection," Liam answered.

"Man. That was really fucking cheesy," Bran said, and Liam shot him an irritated look.

"Not sure how it will work, a hunter and a werewolf," I replied.

"God, Cole, who fucking cares?" Bran asked. "You've never been one to follow the rules and Lord knows, neither is she. You care for her, the whole family sees it, not to mention we all are choking on the sexual tension. So just go and get her, you big douche."

"Wow, he's testy tonight," I said to Liam as he shot a look of annoyance to Bran once more.

"But, he is right," Liam replied. "No matter what happens, you know we will stand by you and her. We would protect her as our own," Liam finished.

I nodded, and I took in my brothers' advice. I stood up, grabbed my keys and went to get the girl.

TWENTY-FIVE

HENNY

After recent events, I tried to relax in my room; however, my nerves wouldn't settle down. I was thankful for Lexi talking to me. She calmed my nerves by offering ideas and suggestions on how the pack could help find my family. I graciously accepted the assistance. Lexi lent me her laptop so I could search the hunter message system for any type of coded messages that could be from my father or Daxon. Nerdy, I know, but it worked in the past.

I remained in my room at the cabin for a majority of the evening, my mind still reeled from kissing Cole, so I tried to keep a low profile. I'm not sure how things were left between us, not to mention Kay was probably leering around, waiting to take my head off.

It had been hours since Cole and I kissed, and he was absent all afternoon. Even though I tried to find news on Dad and Dax, I couldn't get what transpired out of my mind. The memory consistently took me back to that afternoon when Cole caressed my skin, my neck, and my lips. The more I tried not to think about him, the more I couldn't get him out of my head.

My eyes burned from staring at a screen for the last few hours, so I closed the computer to try to sleep. There was a light knock on my door. As I wondered who it was at this time of night, I hoped it was Lexi bringing me some more wine, it would probably help me sleep.

"Come in," I answered quietly, and I stood to meet my visitor. I turned around and stopped up short when I saw Cole leaning against the door frame. He had changed clothes from what he wore earlier. He was now in his signature dark-gray, long-sleeved thermal shirt, dark jeans, and doc martens. How he could make such a simple outfit look incredible was beyond me. His body oozed masculinity. It was incredibly sexy.

I was rooted by his presence, and I suddenly became conscious of what I was wearing. I had dressed in a little pair of sleep shorts and a thin tank top. My hair was in a messy bun scattered on top of my head, and I had traded my contacts for glasses. *Did I have a bra on? Shit.* I didn't. Dragging his gaze all the way up my body, Cole became very aware of my appearance. He pushed off the door frame and moved inside the room. He contemplated his actions for a moment and then turned around to lock the door behind him. Our eyes connected once again, and my nerves were at an all-time high. Cole's eyes held a million emotions in them, and Liam's words floated back to me. *As if fate lets us control who we want?*

"Hi," I said, my whisper barely audible. I knew that he heard me.

Cole still drank me in. I can't remember a time in my life I had been this nervous or this affected by someone. Never in my life had my body reacted the way it does around Cole Martin.

"Hi," he responded. He almost seemed, nervous? Shy? This was not the confident Alpha werewolf I encountered on a daily basis.

"I'm sorry," I blurted. Since I can't control what comes out of my mouth when I'm around him, I continued. "I had no right to get upset over how Kay acted around you. It was completely out of line. I know I haven't exactly been a walk in the park, and I know my earlier actions complicates things. I'm sorry to make things harder for you," *Where did this even come from?*

Cole remained silent as he advanced toward me. It was incredibly unnerving, so I played with the hem of my shirt. Not meaning too, a brief piece of my midriff showed, and when I looked back up at Cole, his eyes were the most electric shade of green. Not to mention his jaw ticked. *Was he angry?* Right now, his body language screamed anger, yet I wanted nothing more than to soothe him.

Cole stalked toward me silently, his eyes moving from my lips back to my eyes. When he reached me, I tried to retreat backward. I couldn't move much before the back of my thighs hit the bed I was just sitting on. He was right in front of me, and my heart moved at an erratic rate. I closed my eyes to calm the nervous edge that his proximity brought.

"Show me your eyes," he said, and my eyes opened at his command. He brushed his hand over my cheekbone, letting it trail down my face as his finger hooked my chin, bringing his lips to mine with the softest contact.

As he pulled away, he shocked me by scooping me up. He turned to sit on the bed, so I straddled him as our kissing continued. Where there was passionate hunger with our kisses earlier, now was just a delicate touch for he treated me with a gentle ease. He trailed away, his breathing just as shallow as mine. Something changed with us today. After finally making physical contact, our connection felt deeper.

"What are we doing?" I asked once again. What if I read too much into Liam's comment about controlling who they want, and Cole didn't feel that way? What if Liam had read his body language wrong? My mind went back and forth the entire evening.

Could I be Cole's mate? We were completely different people from two entirely different worlds. How was this possible? There was one thing I was certain of, in the short time that I knew him, he challenged me, protected me, and fought for me with every fiber of his being. He was the partner I always dreamed of having but never thought I would find.

I was strong and bold, confident and fearless, but at this moment, I was afraid Cole didn't feel the same way. My affections weren't lusting after someone I shared one kiss with. They were deeper, and I needed something more from him. The question I wanted to ask burned on my lips, but I kept quiet.

"I can't stay away from you," Cole replied, his eyes fixed on mine.

"This, between us, this feels so serious. But this is crazy, right? I barely know you." Okay, that did not come out the way I wanted but had the same meaning.

"This is serious," he replied at almost a whisper, and our lips were still a breath apart when he placed his forehead on mine. He deeply breathed me in.

"The first night in the club, I felt it. This electric shock that crossed my body when we touched for the first time. I thought it was a one-time thing, but it happens anytime I'm close to you. Like we're magnets orbiting around one another. That connection isn't normal," my voice was barely audible. I paused to close my eyes and counted to ten before I opened them again. I needed a moment to calm my thundering heart before I asked the question I was dying to know. "It was a mate connection, wasn't it?" I looked up, the green in his eyes was so vivid.

"Yes, you are my mate," he said, conviction in his voice.

I let out a huge sigh of relief that I didn't realize I held in, and it appeared Cole had done the same. Cole leaned in, enveloping me into a warm embrace. This was a Cole I wasn't used to seeing. He was unnerved by this interaction. This was a Cole that was vulnerable and caring. It was the sexiest I'd ever seen him. Heat pooled in my stomach.

As he hugged me tighter, he placed his nose into the crook of my neck and inhaled my scent, placing feather-light kisses on the vampire bite. It was intimate and vulnerable. This was love. *Love.* My heart skipped a beat. I loved Cole. My pulse picked up at the implications of what it all meant, not only for my future but also his. Cole picked up on my anxiety and pulled back. He took my face in his palms. Tears glistened in my eyes.

"We'll never be accepted. They will never accept us," I spoke the truth.

"I don't care, none of that matters to me. You matter. We matter. Besides, my family already adores you," he replied, never breaking eye contact.

"It's not your family I'm worried about," I said, which was the truth. I knew how this ended, I knew what happened in situations like this. It's how my secret was formed. The panic settled in.

"You know nothing about me," I stated.

"It doesn't matter, fate has decided that you belong with me, and I'm going to fight for you with everything that I have. I will fight anyone for you. It's okay, it's all going to be okay," Cole responded.

In that moment, with him, I knew it would be.

TWENTY-SIX

COLE

Last night had been a life-altering experience. As werewolves, we were taught that one day, we would find our mates and life would revolve around them. I had never paid any attention to that until Henrietta Bradford came barreling into my life. Having a mate connection with a hunter was the last thing I would have expected, but here we were. My life revolved around her.

We spent the rest of the night wrapped in each other's embrace. I was worried that it could have gone one hundred different ways, but it didn't. It went the way fate meant it to. I thought of my parents and how happy they would be. My mother would have loved Henny. For the first time in a while, I was relieved.

I had spent a portion of the night going over what a werewolf mating entailed. I gave her a brief overview because I didn't want to overwhelm her. She also talked about their traditions as hunters. The fact that she was bringing that up gave me hope that this would work. After a few minutes of silence, I noticed her breathing had evened out. For the first time in days, she looked at peace, angelic.

Once dawn came creeping in through the window, I eased out from under Henny to make my way back to my room. After spending an entire night next to her in what little she was wearing, I had to keep myself from doing forbidden things to her. I needed to take a cold shower. Hoping that she would rest for a while, I got ready and headed downstairs to talk to my brothers.

Once I made it downstairs, I walked into the kitchen, not expecting to find my family and the entire Atlanta pack in there. Everyone grew silent upon my approach, and it stopped me in my tracks. My eyes connected with Kay, who was seething. Not realizing what had happened, I turned to my brothers. Bran was beaming, and Liam had a look of pride radiating from his face. Then I knew why Kay was so upset. It's possible that with our enhanced hearing, the entire house heard our conversation last night. Kay pushed herself away from the table and went barreling out of the room. I met Landon's gaze with a sympathetic shrug, not knowing what to say when he walked up and slapped me on the back.

"I'll take care of it, man, don't worry about it. Congratulations, buddy."

I nodded to Landon as he exited the kitchen to go after Kay. Liam told me that Landon announced they would be staying with us for a while due to the attack. Nodding to take in the information, I was met again with silence. I sensed Henny's presence enter the room.

Henny was wearing ripped jeans with a gray V-neck t-shirt and a light blue cardigan. She even pulled off the casualness with the pair of white Chuck Taylor's she was wearing. Her blonde hair was in a loose braid, and she was still wearing her glasses. As she noticed us all standing upon her entry, her cheeks blushed and her eyes connected with mine. I couldn't take my eyes off of her.

"Good Morning," I spoke.

Looking at me from under her long eyelashes, she responded. "I'm sorry, I didn't mean to interrupt anything," she said as she stayed by the doorframe as if she wasn't allowed in.

I didn't like her feeling like an outsider, not to mention she was too far away from me. I always forgot how much I need her to be near me until I'm in her presence.

"No, it's okay, come in. Would you like some coffee?" Lexi offered.

Henny nodded with a smile and came further into the kitchen.

"I was telling them what you told me about the messaging system you use with other hunters to communicate. Did you have any luck?" Lexi asked.

But Henny shook her head. "No, there has been nothing," she responded, frustrated.

"Another pack was attacked last night not too far from here. Finn and Mav from Landon's pack were out patrolling when they found out. It was also a group of vampires. We think that they are going after werewolves to get to you. They still think we have you. Also, another set of girls has disappeared," Liam said.

Henny paled as her fists clenched at her sides. "Gareth."

Liam continued. "We think so, but we also think they are trying to turn the groups against each other. The hunters versus the werewolves and vice versa."

Henny walked over to the kitchen sink, grabbing it looking thoughtfully out the window. I could see the tension in her shoulders mounting. Henny took a deep breath and turned to face us.

"We have created a lot of connections with different supernaturals in the different realms. The only problem is that Gareth and I were the ones to set up a lot of those connections, so it's hard to tell who Gareth has in his palm. But, there is a guy I think may be able to help."

"Can we trust him?" I asked.

Henny let out the most beautiful, musical laugh. "Not at all. He's a greedy bastard and will sell anything for the right price. He only looks out for himself. But I think I can talk some information out of him, not to mention, he despises Gareth. So that's in our favor. But, we don't exactly have the best luck when finding out leads," she said as her eyes connected with mine again.

"I'll come with you," I stated. It wasn't a question or hesitation, and Henny nodded.

"We can come, too," Liam countered.

"No, that's okay. My contact is really skittish, if he senses something is up, he'll take off."

Liam and I made eye contact, and I nodded. Sending him a thought to tail back. Telepathy was another one of those werewolf things that Henny would soon learn about, but I hadn't wanted to overload her last night.

"We'll go at dusk," Henny said. "I know where he'll be, Creek's Port."

I nodded, and she walked out of the kitchen, caffeine in hand.

"Creek's Port, huh?" Bran replied. "Care to bring me back some street tacos?"

Henny stopped and looked over her shoulder to respond. "Only if you like them spicy," she smiled slyly and winked.

TWENTY-SEVEN

HENNY

As dusk approached, I made my way downstairs to meet Cole so we could head out to Creek's Port. I neglected to mention to the rest of the pack that Marcus was a troll. I wasn't sure how they would respond. Trolls weren't exactly pleasant beings or that easy to work with. *Oops.*

I waited at the edge of the stairs, and I heard Cole responding to his brothers as he came toward me. Our eyes locked once he stepped into my line of sight. I was caught off guard by his change in appearance. He traded his normal thermal shirt for a black hoodie and his doc martens for Nike's. A flat billed hat sat backward on his head, and it made his green eyes even more vibrant than before. He was so undeniably sexy. He must have recognized the effect he had on me because he smirked, walked over, and placed a soft kiss on my lips.

"You ready?" he asked.

"Yes, Bran and Liam following?" I questioned.

His eyebrows rose in confusion, and he started to backtrack why they were coming.

"It's fine," I answered as I walked away. "We would do the same thing. Let them know to keep a reasonable distance because trolls tend to be a little skittish," I threw over my shoulder on the way to the door. As I looked back, I noticed Cole's reaction, and his eyes narrowed at my confession. I shrugged and blew a kiss at him before going outside.

The ride to Creek's Port was quiet. Cole drove, and I watched the streets of New Orleans pass me by. It didn't feel like the place that I grew up, the place I had protected for so long. It seemed like an entirely different world. One that was filled with chaos and uncertainty. One where I was losing hope.

Wound tight with anticipation, I prepared to meet Marcus. Even though I wouldn't admit it, I was nervous about how this would play out. I didn't think Marcus would fall for Gareth's influences; however, it was imperative to tread carefully as I wasn't certain what side he would align with.

I needed this meeting to go successfully as it would be the closest I would get to information on Dax and Dad. We haven't had the best of luck. As if he sensed my anxiety, Cole reached over and grabbed my hand, placing a feather-light kiss on the inside of my wrist. His eyes remained on the road while his other hand controlled the steering wheel with ease.

Moving his hands to interlock our fingers, Cole's thumb stroked the back of mine, and because my body reacted so well to his, it had a satisfyingly calming effect. Our eyes locked on one another's and we didn't need to say a thing.

We made our way into the city. Cole put his hand out the window to signal to the vehicle behind us to keep going. As the Dodge Ram passed, Liam and Bran nodded in our direction and kept going straight. We pulled up to a dark corner where there was little traffic and shut the truck off. Unable to hide the anticipation of finding Marcus, I tried to leave the vehicle. Cole grabbed my forearm, stopping me from exiting the truck.

"Listen, I know that you're anxious to find information out about your father and brother, but can we please try to maintain a level head about this situation? The last thing we need is you pissing off a troll. Okay? I'm asking very, very nicely," he said as he stroked the back of my hand and looked up at me with bedroom eyes. I sighed at how beautiful he was.

"I'm not always trouble, you know," I said, feigning innocence while trying to hide the fact that he was right, my middle name should have been trouble.

Cole gave me a soft smile. "Well, I have yet to find that out," he responded with a cocky wink.

Once we exited the car, we walked the few blocks to where Marcus would be selling his black-market goods. The weather at this time of night was still stuffy and humid as hell, making sweat stick to the back of my neck. The humidity increased the stink of Creek's Port, which wasn't exactly known for its tourism. Rounding the corner, my eyes connected with a stocky form as Marcus stood in the alleyway, right where I had last seen him. It was almost too predictable, which meant I needed to be smart about this. If this were too easy, it could be a trap. *Again.*

As we discussed before we left the cabin, Cole gave me a nod and went to the back of the alleyway while I made my way to the front. Creek's Port was creepy, and the stench was not enjoyable, so I wanted to get this over with—fast.

"Marcus, Marcus, Marcus," I said, and the troll jumped about ten feet in the air before turning to face me. "I think we have gone over that selling compulsion potions was illegal," I said as I started to lean against the alleyway with my arms crossed over my chest. I would know, considering I succumbed to one not too long ago. "What do you have to say for yourself?"

"Henny! You scared me. And oh God, you're alive! I'm so glad," his beady little eyes darted back and forth, looking for a route to escape. *Silly troll, so predictable.*

His comment about being alive piqued my interest. I cocked my head to the side. "And why wouldn't I be alive, Marcus?"

The troll looked around as he realized his mistake. Marcus was a portly troll who was about two-hundred and fifty pounds, but not any taller than me. He was also about as fast as a sloth. He knew better than to try and outrun me, but he attempted it anyway. *Little shit.*

Marcus turned around and tried to take off when Cole stepped into his line of sight, looking as intimidating as ever while blocking Marcus's exit from the other end of the alleyway. Cole crossed his perfectly sculpted arms over his chest, which only accentuated the muscular nature of his upper body. The moonlight outlined his perfect form, and his green eyes blazed with heated intimidation. He didn't even say a word, but he oozed power. *Yummy.*

Marcus ran back at me, but I had enough. I brought my knee up and plunged it into his stomach. Not hard enough to hurt him but enough to distract him from running. Time was of the essence. He crumpled, fabricating pain, as I brought my foot out and swept his legs from under him. His back fell to the concrete, and I landed on his chest. The weight of my knees kept him immobile, and I used my forearm just to add a little pressure to his neck.

"Why did you think I was dead, Marcus?" I lost my patience. Maybe Cole was right, I was trouble tonight. When he didn't respond, I pressed my forearm a little harder into the scruff of his dirty, greasy hair, cutting off even more circulation.

His eyes turned and pled with Cole. "You're just going to let her do this to me?" Marcus asked. As if Cole would grant him any type of leeway.

"Yeah, I'm good, I'm still too turned on from the way she manhandled you," Cole responded, and it brought a smile to my face.

I winked at him. Power turned him on? I'd have to remember that for later. I pushed a little harder.

"Okay, Okay! Word on the street is that the werewolves are taking out the hunters in New Orleans to gain more territory, but really, it's the vampires. They are trying to gain control of the Southern Province. There is an uprising coming, we hear it in the whispers on the streets," Marcus rushed out.

"I already know that Marcus," I said, annoyed. We learned that much from Jackson.

Marcus went on. "No one has heard from any of the Bradford hunters for days, so it was thought that you all were missing or dead. The remaining hunters are out for blood while the werewolves are not only having to fight the vampires, but now the hunters, too. Your province is doing everything in their power to get to you, to save you from the werewolves."

Cole and I looked up at each other. This wasn't good for Cole's family. If the hunters thought that the werewolves were responsible, this would put a target on the head of every werewolf in New Orleans.

He went on. "I would conclude that you are alive, and with the present company," he looked at Cole, "That may not be the case."

Duh.

"What about Gareth? Have you seen or heard anything from him?" I asked through gritted teeth, fuming about the information I received. I needed to see if anything had come out about Gareth working with the vampires.

"He hasn't been around in days, but it sounds like he's cleaning house around here. Hunters have been more and more present, looking for you guys. This isn't exactly the place to be doing business."

Shit, Gareth may now have a lot of hunters under his influence without them knowing his true intentions.

"Why would the vampires want to gain control of the Southern Province?" Cole asked.

Marcus' eyes flipped back and forth between Cole and me, acting like he was hesitant to answer. I didn't have time for this. I brought my hand up and pinched his ear as hard as I could. Childish, but it did the trick.

"Ow! Ow! The prophecy! The prophecy! The vampires want to take control of the Southern Province so they can try to fulfill the Fae prophecy!"

At that moment, it felt like the world stilled around me. The blood drained from my face, and my heart beat at an erratic rate. *How could Gareth know about the prophecy?* Nobody was supposed to know about the prophecy besides my father, Daxon, and myself. I was in complete shock. If Marcus knew it, others probably did, too.

"Henny?" Cole asked as he picked up on my anxiety.

I looked up at his concern-laced face. Our eyes disconnected when a commotion startled us both. Bran and Liam ran down the alleyway, our attention was now on them.

"We have to go, someone tried attacking the cabin," Liam said quickly.

Cole and I looked back at each other, and I shot up to follow his brothers' retreating forms, leaving Marcus on the ground.

"I will be back! Don't you dare even think about skipping town or telling anyone that I was here!" I shouted at him as I continued running back to the truck, slamming the door shut behind me. Cole stepped on the gas, racing to leave Creek's Port in his rearview mirror.

Speeding down the Louisiana highway, Cole was on high alert and in full Alpha mode. He pulled out his phone and spoke with Bran, who was in the other truck that sped past us. I heard Bran on the other line, confirming that both Lexi and Cassie were okay. *Thank God.* Kay and Landon were on their way back from a patrol when they spotted someone trying to break in. That was the last bit of information Finn had given Bran. We had no idea if there were multiple individuals trying to get in or who it was. Werewolf packs were being attacked all across the province, so it could be anyone. It could be Gareth and his group of rogue vampires.

The drive back to the cabin was quicker than expected thanks to Cole driving in excess of one hundred miles per hour. I understood that

Cole was anxious to get back to protect his pack. I would have done the same for my family.

When we pulled up, Finn was outside, waiting at the door.

"What happened?" Cole shouted as he made his way to the entrance of the cabin. Liam and Bran followed, and I tried to keep up with all of these werewolves. Don't they know I have short legs?

"We're not even sure. Hell, we don't even know how he found this place, you keep it so well protected. But he was fighting to get in, he was fighting to get to her," Finn stopped and directed his eyes toward me.

Finn's statement brought all four werewolves to an abrupt stop. Cole's eyes filled with heated aggression as our eyes locked. I heard stories of the lengths that werewolves would go to protect their mates. I saw the aggression first hand. I would never want to be the one on the receiving end of Cole's anger. I had never felt so protected.

"Where the fuck is he?" Cole turned around and barreled his way into the cabin.

We heard Finn announce that he was in the basement. I tried to keep up with Cole as he flew down the stairs. One thing about Cole was that on a normal basis, he was large, ripped, and full of muscles; but when he transformed into Alpha Cole, he was on another level. He was all Alpha male. It was so sexy. *Reel it in, Henny.*

As we made our way to the edge of the stairs, I barely made out the forms of Kay and Landon, who both looked like they had taken a few hits from the individual tied to a chair in the middle of the room. Trying to look around the guys, the outline of the person made familiarity wash over me. I pushed through them further, getting a better view. I knew that shade of blond hair and the curve of that neck. My heart was about to hammer out of my chest when rationalization took over.

"Oh my God!" I screamed when a pair of ice blue eyes locked onto mine. Ice blue eyes that matched the color and intensity of my own.

Daxon.

160

TWENTY-EIGHT

COLE

Henny pushed past all of us as she ran to her brother in the middle of the room. Relief washed over me when I realized that he wasn't a greater threat.

"Henny!" Daxon shouted in return as Finn and Kay stepped in front of her, trying to stop her.

She barreled right through them and dropped in front of her brother's chair to envelop him in a hug. My adrenaline was still pumping from someone breaking into the cabin. Even now, as she wrapped her arms around her brother's neck, I was seething rage at her touching another male. Liam sensed my aggression.

"Cole, you need to take it down a notch. It's not even like that," Liam whispered.

He was right. I was calming myself as I made my way to the middle of the basement. Henny was pulling away from Daxon and fighting to get his bindings off. She was on the verge of hysteria.

"Oh, thank God, you're okay! I haven't been able to contact you for days. Gareth—" She couldn't get the words out as she choked up on the statement. "Gareth turned against us. I thought he had taken you and Dad. I was terrified you were dead," she spoke so fast I could barely understand what she was saying. Once she had the bindings undone, she pulled him into another hug, but just as quickly pushed Dax away. She placed her hands on his face, searching for injuries.

I was now just noticing the beating he took, probably trying to protect himself from Landon and Kay. It was still unnoticed to Henny.

"Where is Dad?" she asked, worry painted all over her face.

"I don't know," Daxon replied. "Demetri is dead," Daxon said, and Henny flinched at the statement. From what I had heard, Demetri was Jonah's right hand, a partner who would give anything to protect his leader. If Demetri was dead, things didn't look good for Jonah. I cringed at the thought.

"Reed?" Henny asked with pointed anticipation.

"She's fine, they're okay," Daxon responded, and Henny chocked back a sob. I'd never seen her so emotional. "Reed, Nessa, Tate, and Mason, too, we all got out before the shit hit the fan. We don't even know what happened. When we came back to the manor after a false alarm, you were gone and so was one of the Mustangs. We all walked in and next thing we knew, vampires swarmed the place. Dad and Demetri, along with another group, fought them off. He yelled at me to find you and to get the girls out when a group descended on us. There were so many. When I turned around to get Dad, he was nowhere in sight. We fought off all that we could and managed to get out. But it was only then that I saw Gareth stepping out of the manor and had a vampire with him. They seemed too cordial. That's when I knew he was in on this. I went to kill that mother fucker when Reed grabbed my arm, desperate to find you."

The room had gone silent. Both my pack and Landon's had gone completely still from the information while Henny sat in front of her brother in silence. As she was kneeling in front of him, I could see her knuckles turning white under the pressure of gripping them so hard. I was sure that when she opened her hand, blood would flow into her palms from the small, crescent-shaped pattern of her nails. Henny nodded calmly. She turned and stood even straighter and with more confidence than I had ever seen. She stepped in front of Daxon's recovering form and turned around to meet all of us. Her voice was calm and steady but full of malice.

"I understand why my brother is wearing the cuts and bruises. He did try to break into your cabin, but there will be no more instances of him being touched, am I clear?" she said to all of us, but her eyes flashed to Kay. Henny, my five-foot-one Henny, was about to take on five werewolves who threatened harm to her brother. She was fearless. She was irrational. She was reckless. She was mine.

"We're clear," I stated. She and I were locked in one another's gaze, pride radiating off of me. My Alpha female.

She turned back around to Daxon. "Come on," she said. "I have a lot to fill you in on."

As I entered the study, Henny stood looking out the window. Her back was to me, and I could tell from the reflection in the window that she was biting her lip profusely. I wanted to make a comment on how I'd bite that lip for her; however, distress was bouncing off of her aura. It wasn't an appropriate time.

"Are you alright?" I asked.

She turned toward me and swallowed, a blank expression on her face as she was shaking her head to ward off bad thoughts.

"They're dead. They're all dead because of me," Henny said, talking about the hunters in the attack at the manor. I walked to her, placing my palm on her face, trying to soothe her worry.

"Henny, are you in—" Daxon started to say as he walked into the room, and we snapped apart. He stopped at the sight of the two of us, and Henny stepped quickly away from me. He was looking like he had just freshly showered and cleaned up.

Daxon was tall and thin. He was much closer to my height than his sister but was built like a swimmer. From what we had learned from observing the Bradfords, he was the quickest and most agile of them all. Even though he was tall and skinny, he still packed intensity and would be a reputable opponent. Liam definitely did his homework. His short, sandy blond hair matched Henny's, and his eyes were the same ice blue as hers. When they were separate, they didn't really look that similar. But when they were next to each other, they were undeniable. We heard that where Henny was the aggressor, Daxon typically tended to be the mediator. They tended to feed off each other, working better together. "Twin thing", Liam had said. Daxon sauntered his way further into the room and stopped right in front of me. I straightened out, not sure what to expect when he did the last thing I'd thought he'd do, he extended his hand toward mine.

"Thank you for taking care of my sister," he said, his hand still extended.

I took it, giving it a firm shake. "You're welcome," I responded.

There was another knock at the door announcing the entrance of my siblings. They all formally introduced themselves to Daxon, and he returned their introduction, but I noticed that Henny remained silent. Something was off with her. Ever since we had seen Marcus, something had changed.

"How did you find us?" Liam asked, and Daxon and Henny looked at each other. "This place has been in our family for years, it's not exactly listed in the yellow pages. Not to mention how you even found out that your sister was staying with a pack of werewolves."

Henny and Daxon continued to look at each other as if they were sharing an unspoken conversation. Henny took a deep breath and exhaled.

"It's okay," she responded. "We can trust them."

"Henny, I—" but Henny cut him off.

"They need to know," she pleaded and then her eyes shot over to me. Worry coated her features. *What was going on?*

Daxon nodded and turned to face us. "As you know, Henny and I are twins. We share some traits and abilities that enable us to complement one another," he said.

"Yeah, that didn't really tell us anything," Liam responded. The room was quiet with all eyes on Daxon and Henny when she took a deep breath.

"He knows, Dax," Henny said. "Gareth knows."

"How?" Daxon responded, but Henny just shook her head and turned to stand at the window once more, looking outside as if it held all the answers. I was growing impatient. There was something that my mate wasn't telling me, and it was aggravating. Aggravating because she was keeping something from me and aggravating because I didn't know how to protect her. Daxon's face remained impassive.

"Will someone tell me what is happening?" I ground out, and Daxon shot an eyebrow at me.

Henny and Daxon's eyes connected, and she shook her head once again going back to stare out the window. Daxon turned to look at my family.

"The reason that I found out where Henny was is because of the trace that she left through our connection," he stopped as if trying to find the right words, but none of us were following. He took a deep breath and finished his sentence. "The connection that we share through magic."

"Magic?" Bran asked, confused. "Hunters are essentially human, they don't have magic."

"You're right, hunters are not supposed to, but we do."

"Oh shit," Liam said, realization dawning on his face as he turned a shade whiter, just as Henny had done earlier. My impatience was growing, and Henny still hadn't said a word. Like a stone statue, she had remained staring out the window. So, I announced my frustration once more.

"Will someone tell me what the fuck is going on!" I yelled.

The room went quiet, but it was Daxon who spoke next.

"Are you aware of any Fae prophecies?" Daxon asked the room as a whole, but his gaze was directed at me. *Prophecies? Like the one Marcus was referring to earlier?* I perked to attention at his reference of a prophecy.

"Yes," Liam responded. "Our father used to share them with us."

Daxon nodded and continued. We were all completely engrossed in what he had to say.

"There is one, in particular, that is the most prominent of them all. One that affects this realm more than any other. It was prophesied that a descendant of Fae queenship would one day rule over all of the supernatural realms, rightly and just; a fair leader among all. With that power to rule over different realms, they would receive powers from the gods and goddesses in the form of the four elements: earth, wind, fire, and water. It was only after yielding those four elements, the prophesied Fae would be able to control the highest form of magic."

"The Prophecy of the Fates," Cassie responded. Of course she would remember this prophecy, it was her favorite bedtime story because my mother would always reference the chosen one as a female princess. That's what we all thought they were, just bedtime stories.

Daxon continued. "It was known that the most recent King and Queen of the Fae realm were not compatible with each other. Their union was one of convenience. He was greedy, masochistic, and ruled with narcissism while the queen was loving and gentle. The high descendant was the queen as the king prior to that was her father. It was said that while the current king cared nothing for the realm and only concentrated on his greed, the queen became despondent. The queen's guardian grew concerned with her and tried to pull her out of her behaviors; however, something happened that they weren't expecting,"

"They fell in love," Cassie finished, and Daxon nodded confirmation.

"They fell in love."

"As their love was forbidden, they kept any knowledge of their relationship a secret, but their feelings grew more and more for each other. After months of being together, the queen was with child from her guardian's love. Her husband would see this as a betrayal of the highest order, and she was encouraged by her closest maid to end the pregnancy to protect them both. The queen would never do that, she carried out the pregnancy.

"As hiding the pregnancy became more and more difficult, it was finally decided one night that the queen and her guardian would run away to ensure the child was born safely. After that, the queen would return to take the throne, now having a rightful heir to rule after her. On the night she and her guardian planned to run away, they had to stop just outside the city because the baby was coming. The guardian and the queen found a small inn in a tiny Fae village. They believed that the inn would be enough security to stay hidden from the king until after the child was born. The queen, her guardian, and her maid stopped for the night to deliver the child. As the queen pushed, the guardian safely delivered a healthy newborn son; however, she wasn't done. There wasn't only one child in her womb, there were two."

As Daxon's statement, the room went still as his story was starting to fall into place. My breathing hitched. *No, no, no, no, no, no.*

"Once the queen's son was born, the second child that came out was a beautiful baby girl. The queen and her guardian were blessed with twins, the first set of twins in the Fae realm in recent history. The queen knew immediately that something was unique and special about her children. Wanting to ensure their safety, the queen, after just giving birth, decided that they needed to leave immediately. The queen, her guardian, and her twins were nestled to leave. Only it was too late, the king had found them.

"The queen, who had deep magical powers of her own, created a portal to another realm for them all to escape to. In order for her to keep the portal open, she had to be the last to leave. Her guardian was hesitant, and she had to persuade him to take the twins first. The guardian and the twin babies came out of the portal into an unknown realm. The queen professed her love to her guardian, as well as her two newborn children, and closed the portal. She was sacrificing herself to ensure the children were far from the king's reach. While they never found her, word traveled around of the children that were born and that the lost prince and princess are out there. One of them will return with the power of the four elements to save their realm and their kingdom." Daxon finished the prophecy, and the room was as quiet as the dead.

I ran my hands over my face, trying to take in the information overload I just received, and a thought came into my mind. "But don't Fae have distinguishing features that set them apart from—" only I didn't finish my sentence.

I took in Daxon's form. Earlier, his skin was bronze, but it now took on a more translucent hue. His eyes were ice blue before, but now they now blazed aquamarine. The most distinguishing feature that had changed was one that Fae was known to possess. Where rounded ears once stood, Daxon's ears now had pointed tips. Daxon wasn't only a hunter, Daxon was also Fae. My siblings wore the same shocked expression as I did. But if Daxon was Fae than that meant. . .

As if in slow motion, Henny turned around. Right before my eyes, streaks of her beautiful blonde hair turn the softest shade of pink as her skin started to take on that same translucent level as Daxon's. My eyes were relishing in her distinct features as her eyes went from a vivid blue to the most eloquent shade of pink. In that moment, Henny was glowing as she freely let the magic flow through her veins. She looked ethereal.

"It's about you, isn't it?" Bran asked. "You're the lost Fae princess? You're the one from the prophecy." My family remained waiting as Henny's eyes were locked with mine, so many emotions flowed across her face. Fear, longing, anxiety, and love.

"Yes, I'm the lost Fae princess," she answered, her eyes never wavering from mine.

Daxon's voice broke our connection as he continued. "Once our father made it through the portal with us, he ushered us to a sanctuary, which just happened to be a hunter academy. With his glamour and extensive Fae warrior training, the hunters never questioned his abilities when they welcomed him to safety that night. It's not uncommon for fellow hunters to show up unannounced due to trauma or battle, so his arrival was never really investigated. It was that night, our father started his life as a hunter, and ours too in order to better protect our true identities. It didn't take long for the hunters to recognize his strength and abilities as he slowly made his way up the chain of command," Daxon stated as if we needed further confirmation of the prophecy.

Realization hit. My Henny, my mate, was not only a hunter, she was also Fae. Not only Fae but Fae royalty who was slated to rule over the entire supernatural community.

"Holy fuck," Bran choked out.

Yeah, holy fuck.

All eyes were flickering back and forth between Henny and I. Daxon took a step closer to Henny in anticipation that I would act out against her. It was almost laughable, his protectiveness. As if I would harm a hair on her beautiful body. This didn't mean I wasn't upset that she withheld only the most single important bit of information imaginable. Sensing my aggravation at the situation, Henny put her glamour back up, and her blonde hair and blue eyes returned, reminding me of what just happened. My resolved snapped.

"What the fuck, Henny! You didn't think this information would have been important to share with us? To keep you safe?" I shouted.

Both Cassie and Henny jumped at my reaction. I shouldn't have yelled at her like that, but I did.

"She couldn't help it, we've been charmed not to talk about it. It's old magic built to protect us in the event one of us is taken. We can't discuss it unless the other agrees," Daxon said through gritted teeth, his eyes narrowing at me.

"That's why you couldn't talk about what happened when you woke up? The charm prevented you from discussing it?" Liam asked. He had been so quiet I had almost forgotten that he was in the room with us.

Henny nodded at his response. "I told you it was complicated," Henny said to him as she let out a defeated sigh.

They had talked about this?

"Yeah, well it's not exactly uncomplicated when someone yields fire from their hands and barbecues a group of vampires single handily," Bran declared.

As soon as the words left his mouth, he sucked in a breath. *What the fuck were they talking about?* A lot had happened in the last forty-eight hours, and while we hadn't exactly had a sit down to discuss it, this seemed serious. My aggravation had turned to anger from being left out. This was my pack, I was the Alpha. The room had gone unnaturally quiet, and all eyes were now on me. Blood started pumping in my veins, and I couldn't control the tick of my jaw. Trying to calm myself, my fingers were clenching and unclenching so hard against my sides. I was trying not to shift or break my fingers. Not only had Henny been keeping a major secret from me, but it had also looked like Bran and Liam had kept it as well.

I couldn't take it. Moving so quickly, I grabbed a paperweight off the desk and threw it against the wall, causing Henny to startle. As much as I tried to control it, I knew the anger was rolling off of me in waves. Daxon started to step forward, but Liam held out a hand to stop him. Henny's brother or not, anyone who was coming at me right now was getting the reckoning. I needed to leave before I did something stupid, so I turned around and stormed out of the room, breaking free from this entire night.

TWENTY-NINE

HENNY

"Give him a minute," Liam said.

When I turned around, his eyes held a sympathetic gaze.

"He just needs to calm down a little bit, that was a lot of information to process for him, he'll be fine," Cassie stated as she walked over to me and laid her delicate hand on my arm, calming me. Fear started to flow through me. Not only had I kept something from him, but what if he was completely disgusted by what I was? Would he still want to be with me knowing that I essentially had the weight of the supernatural world on my shoulders? Knowing this secret could bring a lot more harm and a lot more chaos. Would he want that?

"He hates it, doesn't he?" I said as I turned to face his siblings.

Daxon took in the surrounding situation with an unguarded expression.

"No, Henny, he doesn't hate it. This just changes everything. This changes the way he is going to protect you," Cassie said, only I didn't quite believe her.

Liam stepped up next to Cassie. "He's probably on his way to the apartment. Bran and I will go talk to him to see if we can settle things. You guys should talk more," Liam said as he motioned between Daxon and me.

I nodded a thanks as Liam and Bran walked out of the room.

"I'll let you two get settled," Cassie said as she turned to my brother. "I'm glad you're okay, Daxon. Henny was really worried about you."

"Thank you," Daxon responded, and Cassie exited the room leaving Daxon and me together.

I folded my arms over my chest and let out a breath I hadn't even realized I was holding. When I turned to Daxon, he donned a big, stupid grin on his face, and I immediately narrowed my eyes.

"What?" I said annoyed. No less than two hours ago, I had been worried he was dead. Now, he was right back to annoying me. *Siblings.*

"Nothing, apparently I'm not the only one who isn't up to date on the most recent events. I would really love to hear how you have not only come in contact with a pack of werewolves but care about the thoughts of its Alpha. Henrietta Bradford doesn't give a shit about what anyone thinks, let alone a guy. Your body language sure said more about Cole's reaction. The guy seems like an asshole if you ask me."

I stood there, biting my lip and tapping my toe, trying to ponder how I would relay all of this information to Daxon. My hand started to play with my chain. As if reading my mind, like he always does, he answered.

"Just start from the beginning, Hen."

So, I did.

I laid out each and every detail that happened from the moment I found out about Gareth's betrayal until I came back to the cabin and found Daxon there. I didn't go into detail about the mate connection with Cole as I didn't think he would have been able to handle that. I would need to figure out how to tell him soon as he had already sensed something was going on between us. As if I could hide anything from him for that long anyway. He wasn't happy about how I reacted to Cole, but he was grateful that his family had kept me safe.

After hours of discussion, Daxon said he needed to get word out to Reed that he was okay, and then he was going to crash for a few hours before we figured out a way to connect with the others. In order to remain safe, they were not close by. At the mention of her name, another wave of relief washed through me. They were all okay. If only I had information about my dad.

After Dax had laid down on one of the love seats in my room, I thought about how Cole reacted when there was a knock at the door. I shot up hoping it was Cole but deflated when I answered and found Bran leaning against the doorframe, looking as casual as ever. Before I could even get a word out, Bran spoke.

"Come on, let's go for a ride," he said.

I knew where he was taking me. I looked back at Dax's sleeping form. He crashed shortly after we talked, and I could tell he had been plagued with exhaustion, not to mention, he was in a fight with werewolves. He probably would sleep for a while.

"He'll be fine," Bran said, picking up on my hesitation. "Lexi and Liam will be here if he needs anything, and he'll be able to get a hold of you. He's back, Henny, we're not going to let anything happen to him. You're one of us now."

In all of the interactions that I had with Bran, this was the time he'd been most serious. He was telling the truth, they would protect Dax and me endlessly.

"Thank you," I replied, a little choked up.

I slowly shut the door behind me and followed Bran to his truck. The ride was quiet, and I appreciated the silence. It gave me time to think about what I wanted to say. Bran pulled the truck up to the curb of Cole's apartment and waited for me to exit. I looked over at Bran, and he showed no motion to get out of the vehicle.

"You're not coming with me?" I questioned, and Bran laughed.

"Ah, no. You're on your own. Apartment is the third floor, last door on your left. The door is unlocked."

I narrowed my eyes at him. "Traitor," I spat out, but he only smiled at me. I took a deep breath and went up to Cole's apartment. As Bran said, the door was open, and I let myself in. I locked the door behind me and leaned against it as I took a calming breath.

The apartment was dark and quiet. I looked around as I remembered the first time I had been here. It looked more peaceful in the dark of the night as I could hear the nightly sounds of the city in the background. I took a deep breath, inhaling the scent of Cole. In the distance, I heard the shower running, and I made my way into the living area of the studio apartment. I sat down on the couch and looked out the window at the Louisiana night sky.

From the apartment, everything looked so normal, so natural. The world didn't know that a supernatural war brewed and it would affect them all. I was so deep in my thoughts that I didn't hear Cole approach, but I sensed his presence. I gathered the strength to look at him as he walked further into the room, and I now felt him right behind me. I took a deep breath and stood, getting ready to explain myself when I was halted in my place unable to speak.

Having freshly showered, Cole wore nothing but a pair of jeans, which were draped blushingly low on his hips, accentuating the v-line that every woman lusts over in a man. As if in slow motion, my eyes traveled over his perfectly sculpted abs and muscular chest. My gaze stopped for a second on the Alpha mark on his ribs. I felt the heat from the hot water as it radiated off of him. Droplets of water that he missed while drying his hair dripped seductively down his neck, begging to be licked off.

His hands were placed casually in his pockets; however, the relaxed nature still accentuated the ripped muscles of his forearms and biceps. My eyes continued to travel their way up to his shoulder muscles, and I had an immediate flash of grabbing them as I was withering beneath him. My gaze finally connected with Cole's, and his eyes held a determined shade of green as if he were challenging me not to come closer to him.

Completely entranced, I stepped to him, still holding my breath. When I had walked into the apartment, I was ready to stand my ground and explain that he had no right to be mad at me, only I did the exact opposite. When a shirtless Cole Martin was involved, I was putty in his hands. I expected him to be enraged, but he wasn't. He was the complete opposite; he was tender.

As if two magnets pulled us together, we were now a breath away from each other. The mate connection buzzed with electricity as our bodies nearly touched. This was the first time that we were alone, really alone, since the night he saved me. My heart rate increased.

Facing each other, I slowly caressed his biceps and trailed my fingers down his forearms until my hands rested on his naked hips. I pulled him closer to me so that we connected. An appreciative rumble escaped from his lips, telling me that he liked was I was doing. *Did he just growl?* I didn't care, whatever noise he made, it was sexy as hell.

"I'm sorry," I whispered against his lips. "I never intended to keep you in the dark, I never meant to—"

He interrupted me. "It's okay, I shouldn't have reacted the way I did. It's just, fuck, Henny. I wasn't expecting that to come out. This complicates things, a lot. If this gets out any more than it already has, it could mean a lot of people coming to look for you, for us. I was scared because, for the first time since I met you, I was worried that I wouldn't be enough to protect you."

Cole's confession caught me off guard. Out of everything that he felt, that was not what I expected. I thought he harbored anger for being lied to and misled. But when all was said and done, all he worried about was my protection. I brought my hand up and placed it on his cheek. He leaned into it, closing his eyes. I brought myself even closer to his face, running my nose against his.

"I was worried that after you found out I was Fae, you wouldn't want anything to do with me anymore," I confessed. It was all I could think about.

He grabbed my face in his hands. "As if you could do anything that could make me not want you, Henny. These emotions I feel for you, they're so strong. All my life, my father prepared us for what it would be like when we had our mate connection, but even after being prepared, it's a thousand times stronger than I expected. I was worried that with the intensity of my feelings, you wouldn't want me. But it doesn't matter; where you go, I follow. When you're worried, I want to ease those worry lines from your pretty little face. When you're hurting, I will fucking ruin anyone who caused you pain. You're it for me, Henny. I know it hasn't been very long, and this is complicated, but I love you. I love you so fucking much that—"

I cut him off by crashing his lips to mine. At his confession, I needed to be connected with him in every way possible. I felt the same way Cole did, but he was the first one to verbalize it. After everything he learned about me, and everything that could possibly be coming down the road, he didn't care. He still wanted me anyway.

As soon as my lips met his, my entire body was on fire, lighting up brighter than the fourth of July. I eagerly wrapped one arm around Cole's neck and used my other to pull the waistband of his pants closer to me so that his hips touched mine. Both of his strong hands moved into my hair, pulling our lips closer than ever before.

Slipping my tongue into his mouth, I continued to kiss him as I bit down on his lower lip. He growled once more and picked me up around the waist one-handed. I wrapped my legs around his hips, and before I knew it, we made our way to the bed. Our lips never broke contact.

We stopped at the edge of the bed, and Cole gently set me down and kneeled so my legs were open to his hips. His mouth moved from my lips to the sensitive spot behind my ear, moving tantalizingly slow down my neck only to stop to nip at my collarbone. I let out a breathless moan.

As his mouth went back to mine, his fingers explored their way down my chest and landed on the button on my jeans. Cole only pulled away from the kiss to look at me, asking permission. Since I couldn't form a coherent thought, all I did was let out a listless nod, and our kissing continued.

Popping the button of my jeans, Cole slowly lowered the zipper and played with the hem of my waistband, his lips going back to mine. It was almost embarrassing how much I gasped for his touch. As if sensing my need, Cole slipped his fingers into my panties.

Cole's fingers explored my body, reaching the spot I was so eager for him to delve into. His thumb worked expertly as he slipped a finger inside of me, and I almost combusted at the contact. All I could do was grip his shoulders and moan breathlessly into his mouth. His fingers worked with expert precision and the tension built inside of me.

"Fuck, you're tight," he said as he growled into my mouth and his fingers continued their swift movements. I lifted my hips for him, guiding his fingers deeper, making him rumble with appreciation.

With his other hand going to my hair, he seductively pulled at my nape, so I was forced to open to him, and he ran his nose along the base of my neck.

"This is the spot you know," he whispered into the space where my neck met my shoulders. "This is the spot where a werewolf officially marks his mate." My heart stopped at his confession.

At his words, my body was taken to an even higher level of arousal as his fingers began to move faster and faster. I felt the ball of tension building between my legs and my moans became more frequent, much to Cole's satisfaction.

"That's it, let it go," he whispered. As if his words were a command, I broke apart as his lips met mine again. He trailed his tongue over my lower lip as I was still reeling from the high he had just given me.

Biting my lip, I was overwhelmed with the urge to touch every inch of his body, to give him the satisfaction he had just given me. I stood up, pushing him away from me as I guided him to sit on the bed. I slowly prowled toward him, and his carnal gaze met mine. I lowered myself down to my knees, so we were face to face and brushed his lips with the gentlest touch.

Following the same movements he had done to me, I slowly unbuttoned his jeans and lowered his zipper. When I noticed he wasn't wearing underwear, I bit my lip while my inner vixen squealed with delight.

Ever so slowly, I lowered his jeans as his hard length sprang free. Bringing my lips to his neck, I took him in my hands and slowly caressed him. His breathing increased the faster I stroke. My lips explored his body.

"Shit Henny, that feels so fucking good," he said passionately as his hands went back into my hair. Slowing rising from his body, my eyes joined with his as I positioned myself even lower between his open legs. His breathing became ragged, and his eyes furiously followed my lips when I opened my mouth and took him in completely. Gripping the edge of the bed with his hands, Cole hissed a string of profanities as he dropped his head back. His arousal encouraged me further, so I took him into my mouth deeper. Feeling an overwhelming urge of satisfaction flow through me, I picked up the pace, developing a sensuous rhythm.

The entire time, Cole's eyes were completely on mine. Having him watch me work him was the most erotic sensation I had ever felt. Pulling him out of my mouth, I grabbed his base and ran my tongue from top to bottom, much to his liking.

"Yeah baby, keep going," he whispered.

I took him in my mouth again, picking up the pace. As small twitches came across Cole's body, I knew he was getting close. I moved faster, sucking harder. The only time Cole broke eye contact with my lips was when he closed his eyes for a few seconds, trying to collect himself. He was getting ready to go over the edge.

"Henny, you gotta stop, I'm getting close and if you keep going—"

Only I didn't stop, I kept going. I shoved my mouth down harder capturing him completely. At that action, Cole shouted as his creamy substance filled my mouth entirely. Never in my life had I felt sexier than at that moment. Looking up at him, I swallowed every last drop.

As Cole came down from his high, his eyes met mine again, and I gently pulled away tucking him back in. He immediately pulled me close to him, so we were inches apart and placed the softest kiss on my lips.

"You're going to be my undoing," he whispered into my mouth before his lips met mine again. I knew exactly what his words meant because Cole Martin wasn't going to be my undoing, I was already undone.

THIRTY

COLE

Henny and I lay tangled in a heap on my bed for the next few hours. As clichéd as it sounds, earlier tonight was one of the best nights of my existence. I've been reeling from Henny's presence, and finally feeling her touch was the sweetest thing I could have imagined. It wasn't just about the act itself, it was about her smell, her touch, her taste.

"What are you thinking about?" Henny asked, bringing me back to the present.

I turned to look down at her, and her rose-colored Fae eyes were staring back at me. I ran my fingers just under her cheekbones. Her skin turned a shade of scarlet as she blinked. When she opened them back up, they were blue.

"No, don't," I said. "They're beautiful." I brought my fingers down her cheek again. "You're the most beautiful thing I've ever seen."

She leaned into my touch and her eyes were blush colored once more.

"Stop distracting me, what are you thinking about?" Henny asked again.

"Just thinking about our next steps," I lied, and she nodded in response.

"Hmmm," she responded thoughtfully.

I dug my face into the crook of her neck and laughed. "You think that after what we just did, I'm thinking about next steps?" I asked her, and she giggled in response. She actually giggled, it was the most melodious sound I'd ever heard. My lips touched hers when my phone pinged, bringing us back to reality.

Henny sighed in disappointment.

"We have to go," I said.

A look of concern flashed over her face. "Is everything okay?" she replied.

"Yeah. Daxon is up, and they are asking for you."

"They?" she questioned in confusion.

"Yes, they," I said. "Your friends are there."

We drove back in silence; my hand was locked onto hers. I could tell Henny was nervous because she was biting her lip and staring out the window.

"Does your brother know about us?" I asked. Better to get that out of the way instead of it getting brought up in a room full of hunters. Henny gave me a sideways glance and bit her lip even further.

"To an extent," she sighed and turned to face me. "I didn't get into the complete specifics of it," she said with a pleading look like she thought I would be upset that she didn't share the whole truth. She had been worried about it from the beginning and made it clear her family would never accept us.

"Hey, it's okay," I said. "We'll figure it out."

She gave me a soft nod and smile.

The cabin looked the same from the outside, but I could tell the atmosphere had changed. Their presence was everywhere. As I exited the vehicle, Henny shot around and stepped right in front of me, her blush eyes and hair still intact.

"They don't know the extent of everything, Cole. The prophecy. Just you and your family, we have to tell them." she said, and just like that, her glamour went back up.

I understood. "Nothing will happen to you, Henny. I will always protect you. Even if it's from your own," I said. It was true, I would fight her family if it ensured her safety.

"I know, and they would never hurt me but thank you," she said as she grabbed my hand and gave it a small squeeze. But she sighed, her jaw was still ticking as she was playing with her fingernails. Not letting her hand go, I pulled her right to me, so she was flush against my chest, our lips nearly touching.

"Is that why you are still so nervous?" I asked.

She looked up at me, the moonlight dancing on her skin. Taking in her appearance, I could hear nothing but the calm Louisiana breeze and the sounds of the forest around us. It would be peaceful, had it not been for the circumstances of why we were there.

"Kinda. . ." she said as if trying to gauge my reaction. "The other hunters who are there; Nessa is mated to Tate, and Reed and Daxon have been in love with each other since they could walk," she continued her assault on her lip.

"Okay?" I wasn't understanding why this was such a big deal.

"Well Mason is with them," she answered, another deep breath escaping from her. "He and I had a small thing. A *very* small thing. It didn't last long at all, there was nothing there, no spark. But since tonight was all about honesty. . .full disclosure."

And there it was, that's why she was so nervous. I tried to control my breathing as a newfound ferocity came over me. I knew Henny had a life before me, but still, the thought of someone else touching her in the same intimate way that I had just touched her made me want to go berserk. I sent a mental thought to Bran and Liam to have them with me when I met Mason. I looked into the vast darkness of the forest, trying to calm my anger.

"Cole?" she questioned.

"Give me a minute," I said, closing my eyes trying to calm myself down. Just standing here in her presence was helping, but I couldn't get the thought of her with someone else out of my head. The tingles I got when I was ready to shift were flowing, and my breathing grew labored. That's the downside of being not only a werewolf, but an Alpha werewolf. The switch can flip at any moment. I met her gaze and shrugged my shoulders.

"Okay, I'll just go in there and break his nose," I said nonchalantly. That earned me a punch in the arm. *Holy fuck that hurt, ow.* She was smiling, the nervous energy that was once radiating from her was gone, and that brought me back down, too. In a matter of seconds, she had calmed me.

"You're not going to punch him, it was literally years ago," Henny responded, trying to hide the smirk that was now on her face.

"Do you remember meeting Kay King?"

Henny narrowed her eyes at me. "First of all, Kay is awful. Second of all, no one decided to tell me that this mating thing was going on, which was why my feelings were amplified by a thousand and a third," she said as she went on her tiptoes, placing her lips right by my ear, causing goosebumps to erect on my skin, "Don't touch what's mine."

My wolf purred in delight.

"By the way," she said as she kissed the side of my temple and leaning into my body. "I love you, too."

THIRTY-ONE

HENNY

As I made my way inside Cole's cabin, a red blur crashed into me before I fully entered the house. I returned her embrace.

"Oh my God! I was so worried about you," Reed cried as tears streamed down her face.

She had almost taken me down with the force of her hug but I didn't care, I met her intensity and hugged her back. I wasn't sure I would ever see her again. "I'm so glad you're okay," I said as I pulled her back to get a good look at her.

Reed had puffy red eyes like she had been crying, and her nose sounded nasally like she had a cold. Daxon had said that she was so happy we were okay that she couldn't stop. Typical Reed, she was so emotional. While it was something she was often embarrassed about, it was one of the things I loved most about her.

"Me too," she replied as she pulled back, her hands resting on my shoulders. She just sat there for a moment looking at me.

"Okay, this is weird, stop staring at me," I said, and we both laughed.

"I know! I'm sorry," she said as she patted my cheek adoringly.

"She's been a piping hot mess since you've been gone," Nessa added as she made her way to me, and my smile grew even bigger. Giving me a soft hug of her own.

Nessa and I weren't as close as Reed and I, but she was still a very dear friend. She would do anything for me and vice versa.

"So glad you are okay," she responded.

I smiled and as they both stepped away, they awkwardly stared behind me. Nessa had her eyebrow raised. I remembered that Cole was behind me during Reed's ambush, staying silent to not interrupt the moment. He knew what they meant to me. My cheeks reddened, and I turned around to look at him. He casually leaned against the door frame with his hands in his front pockets, his legs crossed at his ankles, and his eyes still on me. My mind instantly went to how I found him in a similar position earlier. My blush deepened even further at the memory.

"Oh, I'm sorry. Umm. . .Reed and Nessa, this is Cole. He is my. . .," I stopped myself. *Oh God.* "Um, it was his family who found me the night of the vampire attack. Cole, these are my best friends," I said as I turned to Reed, squeezing her hand. "They are my family," I said, causing tears to escape from Reed again. I shook my head smiling. She was so cute.

As I turned around to further acknowledge the introduction, Cole looked like a Greek god standing there so casually in the dim light of the hallway. Wearing his signature boots, jeans, and thermal shirt, he needed nothing more. A charming smile sprouted across his face.

"It's a pleasure to meet you, ladies," Cole said as he nodded his head respectfully. "Henny has been really worried about all of you. I'm glad everyone is safe," he replied with the most charismatic nature I had ever seen.

I wasn't used to seeing him with this type of attitude. I got the defensive and protective werewolf, but Reed and Nessa got the delectable charmer. Bewitched by his charm and good looks, Reed and Nessa fawned over the introduction.

"Well a thank you is also in order to you for keeping her safe," Reed responded as she batted her eyelashes at Cole, twirling a piece of her red hair.

If Daxon were here, it would be a different story, and I rolled my eyes at the sentiment. I knew that gesture wasn't anything romantic, but it was a sign that she approved of Cole when she turned and beamed at me. Cole nodded and smiled again, stepping forward to lead us to where everyone else was in the living room. As he walked away, Reed rushed over to my side and looped my arm through hers.

"Oh my God, he is sexy!" Reed whispered in my ear, only it didn't matter that she whispered.

I narrowed my eyes at her, she did that on purpose. With Cole's hearing, he would have heard her anyway. Cole turned his head to me briefly and winked. Apparently, if there was the matter of Cole and I being together, Reed and Nessa approved.

We made our way to where everyone was. Cole's pack came into view along with Daxon and the guys. What once was a large living area, now seemed small with all the supernatural bodies that occupied it. Cole made his way over to his brothers when Liam whispered into his ear. Cole bit his lip as if to calm himself when I turned around and collided with a muscular chest.

I pulled away to find that Mason stood right in front of me. His tall and lean frame was built like Daxon's. I looked up to take in his blond hair and hazel eyes. He had his hands on my shoulders to steady me, his million-dollar smile shining back at me.

Mason was what I would define as the true, all-American boy. He was typically the face of the hunters as he is loyal beyond reason, definitely being the most admirable one out of all of us. He worked government relations with the different provinces, so he traveled a lot. He was a rule follower, through and through. While Mason would have been a valuable partner, we would have never worked out. I was defiant, aggressive, and audacious; while he was sweet, loyal, and devoted. I needed someone strong and passionate. I needed someone who was brash and confident. I needed Cole.

"Hey, Mason. I'm glad you guys are okay," I responded as I started to step away from him. He looked a little hurt by my lack of contact, but I was more concerned with Cole. Looking in his direction, he gripped the edges of the table in the ultimate stare-down with Mason, who remained completely oblivious. He was taking this a lot better than the first time I met Kay. One thing that Cole did mention the other night was that werewolves were overly protective of anyone who touched their mates. I knew he struggled to maintain control. I needed to sooth the tension that flowed through his body.

I wandered in Cole's direction when Tate gave me a punch in the arm, signifying without words that he was glad that I was okay. Being the only mated pair in the bunch, Nessa and Tate matched each other perfectly. Nessa's brown hair and tanned skin complimented his blacker than night locks and lighter tone. Both of their eyes were chocolate brown. He nodded in my direction and placed a small kiss on Nessa's temple before wrapping his arm around her shoulder.

Turning around, Cole had also moved closer to me, and we now stood side by side. His mere presence brought an air of calmness to me. Even though we weren't touching, our connection buzzed, pulling us together with an invisible thread. I shook my head to rid the haze he created. Glancing out of the corner of my eye, he suppressed a smile, telling me he knew exactly what his presence did to me. *Stupid werewolf.*

"Thank you, everyone, for coming," Liam stated, commanding everyone's attention. "A lot has happened over the last few days that affects us all, so it's important that we talk everything through. Henny and Cole, why don't you detail everything that has happened."

Over the next few hours, I told my hunter family everything they needed to know. Their mouths hung agape when Daxon and I informed them of the prophecy and our relationship to it. I knew Daxon was going to tell Reed in private, so she was already aware of it. The only thing I didn't really elaborate on was the exact extent of my relationship with Cole. That was a conversation that would be best saved for a later time. As we finished, we were met with stunned silence at Gareth's betrayal. They had known him just as long as we had.

"We haven't really had luck in our corner. We don't know how far Gareth's reach extends. Looking into different leads has not gone well. Not only that, but it seems that he is pitting supernatural groups against each other as a distraction," Liam said.

We needed to find out more, but first and foremost, we needed to find my dad.

"I have an idea," Daxon spoke up.

"Please, by all means," Liam responded.

Daxon turned in my direction with a look of apprehension across his face. "I think I have an idea, but I'm not sure you're going to like it. I'm almost positive it would help us find information on Dad."

"What are we even waiting for?" I asked, waiting for him to spit it out. If it would help Dad, I don't know why he didn't say it sooner.

"Well, it would involve a trip to Turner's," Daxon responded with a look of displeasure on his face.

Understanding went through me. *Yikes.* This was another poor decision coming to bite me in the ass.

"What's at Turner's?" Cole asked, immediately looking in my direction.

Turner's was a hole-in-the-wall-type bar but definitely not like the one I visited with the werewolves.

"A seer that I think I can trust. Gareth always had a distaste for the seers, so I don't think he would have gotten through to them. Although, it might take a little bit of sweet talking for her to help us," Daxon said as he arched an eyebrow at me, showing that it was my fault. Oh, she would need to be sweet talked.

"Care to elaborate?" Cole questioned.

"Well, last time we were there, Henny just happened to punch her in the face," Daxon said.

Bran barked out a laugh. Cole once again suppressed a smile as he folded his arms over his chest.

"That seems to happen a lot around here," Cole said to me as he cocked his head to the side. Man, I loved when he did that. It almost took the embarrassment out of his statement. His gaze had me squirming as I placed my hands on my hips.

"I'm sorry, but groping my brother while I was standing right there was a bit uncalled for and a bit of whorish. If anything, I taught her a lesson on how to act more like a lady."

Reed snickered from behind me. She heard the story, and she was completely supportive of my actions.

This time it was Daxon who laughed out loud. "Whatever you say, Hen House," Daxon responded.

I cringed at the use of the nickname he had for me. He'd been using it since we were kids. If Bran had thought the conversation was entertaining before, he absolutely lost it now, rolling with laughter.

"Oh, Hen House!" he said between breaths. "I can't handle it!"

I groaned at the conversation and just wanted to get it over with.

"Can we please just go to Turner's?" I asked as we all huddled together, coming up with a plan.

THIRTY-TWO

COLE

Last night and most of this morning had been spent debriefing and coming up with a plan for later. I was leaning against the doorframe of Henny's room as I watched her scramble to prepare for their trip to the seer. My arms were crossed over my chest in an open display of aversion to this entire fucking idea. It seemed to go unnoticed by Henny, which was only aggravating me more. Henny and Daxon announced that it would be best if it were just the two of them who went to speak with the seer. It was an attempt to get in her good graces, not to mention, a lot of people may draw attention.

"I don't like this," I said as I expressed my aversion for the plan for the millionth time.

Henny just waved me away once more. God, she was so damn stubborn. I hated that she wouldn't relent, but at the same time, I loved the courage she had to fight for what needed to be done, not only for her family but for mine. I was still heavily conflicted. I could feel my jaw ticking, and the muscles in my neck were tightening. The thought of her going into a situation where I couldn't help her made me restless.

As if sensing my discomfort, Henny walked over to place a hand on my chest, batting her beautiful, long eyelashes at me. "It's going to be fine. If anything, I'm going to come back with a broken nose of my own," Henny replied as she tried to lighten the mood.

It wasn't working. I sighed and pinched the bridge of my nose. "Henny, we don't know if anyone, any place, or any person is safe right now. Even if the seer agrees to speak to you, what if Gareth has someone watching the place? I don't like taking that risk," I said as I addressed my concerns. "I've said it before, I won't risk you."

Henny moved my hand from my nose and put both of her palms on either side of my face. I had no other choice but to look at her. "I think you're forgetting that I have spent the last twenty-two years of my life training to protect myself in situations such as this. I have to do something, Cole. I can't idly stand by while something could be happening to my father. You know I'm not that kind of girl," she answered with conviction.

I knew she was right, if it had been my father I would have done anything to get him back. I pulled her into a tight hug, inhaling her beautiful scent of wildflowers and fresh rain. It smelled just like home. "I know," I said. "It's just if anything happens to you—" I couldn't finish that statement.

"Nothing will," she responded as she rubbed her nose along my neckline.

I kissed her temple and hugged her a little harder. "If you keep nuzzling me like that, you won't be going anywhere for a few hours," I said as she had pulled back to look up at me, her cheeks were painted with the rosy color I had grown to love.

"It's going to be okay," she said as she ran her hands down my chest to rest on my heart. "And when I come back, I'll show you just how okay it is." I didn't have time to respond to that comment as she pressed her lips to mine.

THIRTY-THREE

HENNY

Shortly before midnight, Daxon and I made our way down a deserted street to Turner's. The humidity hung heavy in the air as the fog slithered through the streets of New Orleans, making this walk much more hair-raising than normal. Black iron street lamps cast an eerie glow onto the street, causing an abnormal shade of orange to resonate into the surrounding area. One thing that this area was known for were the ghosts that lingered around at night, attempting to resolve unfinished business. I really hoped that I wasn't subjected to an unwelcomed visit. There were not many things that I was afraid of, but ghosts scared the shit out of me.

We choose to leave later in the evening, attempting to remain as inconspicuous as possible. I immediately regretted that decision as I felt the hair on the back of my neck stand at attention while we made our way to Turner's.

"Damn, Hen, slow down. If you walk any faster, I'll be running," Daxon expended, sounding out of breath.

But, I kept up my pace. The sooner we got there and out of the dark, moving shadows of the alleyways, the better. "I don't care, Daxon. Keep up, you know this area creeps me the hell out," I responded.

He let out a chuckle. "Ah, I forgot. The resident fated princess, supernatural badass, and all-time pain in my ass is afraid of ghosts," he gaffed as I narrowed my eyes at him.

"Not afraid, indifferent." *I was totally afraid.*

"Whatever you say, princess," Daxon finished as we finally arrived at Turner's.

"You good?" he asked, and I nodded. At my nod, Daxon opened the door.

Turner's looked exactly the same as the last time I was here. There was one lone patron that sat near the end of the bar, and one bartender, who made eye contact with my brother.

"Bradford. Haven't seen you around in a while," the bartender, who I believed was named Tex, said lackadaisically.

"Yeah, things have been a little crazy," Daxon responded as Tex raised an eyebrow at him.

"So I've heard."

Well, that wasn't good. At his response, my entire figure was on alert. If there had been rumors of what was going on, then someone may have already been here. *And Cole would have been right.* As if gauging the situation, Daxon went right to the point.

"Is she here?" he asked.

Taking in a moment of contemplation, Tex nodded. "Although, I'm not sure how happy she'll be that your twin came along," he said, and I rolled my eyes.

Daxon smiled. "I think we'll be fine. Thanks, Tex," Daxon replied as he tapped his knuckles on the wooden bar and made his way back to the stockroom.

I nodded my gratitude and followed suit. We went behind the back of the building, and I followed Daxon through the hallway that led to a set of darkened stairs. As we descended, I was hit with the aroma of burning incense. Once we reached the bottom of the steps, I turned to a small area that was decorated with an array of red and black ensembles. Two red lounge chairs and a black loveseat stood out against the charcoal walls that had painted-on stars. Candles burned and cast a soft, yellow glow over the alluring blonde, who was sitting in the lounge chair closest to us. Her body stiffened, and her eyebrow rose as she took me in.

"Leighton, it's been a while," Daxon acknowledged. "We were hoping that you could help us."

"I know," she answered disinterested. "I think that you are forgetting that I saw this coming. Henrietta," she said as she threw a satiated gaze my way.

"Leighton. Good to see you, your face looks great by the way." *AH! That did not come out right.* "I mean, looking beautiful as always," I tried to retract, as I heard Daxon curse next to me.

"Thanks," Leighton responded through gritted teeth.

Daxon threw a narrowed gaze in my direction, and all I could do was shrug, which made Daxon roll his eyes.

"Leighton, please, Jonah is in trouble. We could really use your help to find anything out. Even the smallest piece of information could be a clue."

At Daxon's statement, her body language and gaze softened a little bit. "I know," she responded. "There have been rumors floating around. Dark days are coming. But if I'm going to help," she spoke up a little louder. "Might as well have the werewolves join us."

What did she just say?

At her statement, two heavy sets of boots descended down the stairs, and Cole and Bran came into view. I placed a hand on my hip, sending him a narrowed gaze. He just came over and stood by my side without saying a word. Our pinky fingers brushed lightly as a spark of electricity went through my hand at the contact. In reality, I couldn't be mad at him for coming. I did the same thing at the warehouse, blatantly disregarded what he said to ensure he was safe.

Leighton observed our interaction with curiosity. Had she seen our future, or how our relationship developed? Leighton wasn't the only one to observe us. Daxon's eyes were on us before he turned back to Leighton. Leighton's voice broke my attention.

"You aren't going to throw up on my carpet, are you?" she asked snidely. *What the hell was she talking about?* As I turned to inquire about the brass statement she just made, I noticed she wasn't looking at me, but at Bran, who remained rooted at the bottom of the stairs. He looked an unusual shade of green, and a sheen layer of sweat broke out over his forehead. His eyes were locked on Leighton's. I've never seen him so unnerved.

"Is that going to be a yes or a no? Because if you are, I'm really going to need you to take it outside," Leighton said flatly.

There was still no response from Bran.

"Bran?" I asked. I was worried for his wellbeing. When there was still no response, I looked over at Cole to ask him to do something. He was grinning like the Cheshire Cat. *What the hell?* As if finally broken from his spell, Bran silently moved to stand next to Cole and remained silent the entire time.

"Yeah, that was weird," Daxon said as his gaze went between Bran and Leighton. "Right, Leighton, if you will."

Leighton nodded. "Henny and Daxon, I need you to take the two seats directly across from me. As you are Jonah's descendants, I might be able to get a stronger connection if you two join hands. It will also work in our favor that you two have a twin bond. We're not sure why they are stronger so don't ask. Just know this isn't an exact science so most of the time I don't know what the hell I'm doing."

Daxon and I looked at each other before we took the seats that Leighton instructed. Cole stood an arm's length behind my chair, ready to be there if needed. Bran remained rooted in his spot as if in a daze. *Yeah, definitely going to need to see what that is about.*

Leighton sat down on the loveseat and blew out a few candles, only to light a lone turquoise one on the small coffee table between Daxon and me. The room cast an eerie teal glow.

"What's the significance of teal?" Cole asked.

"It's my favorite color," she replied as she rolled her eyes at him. *Um, okay.* She sighed in annoyance. "Sometimes our magic flows easier when we are in the presence of things that calm us, things we enjoy."

That answer seemed to pacify Cole, and he nodded.

"Very well," she started. "I need you to clear your minds, and both of you need to picture the last time that you interacted with your father. Try to concentrate on everything you remember about that moment. The sights, smell, touch, it's all important. That is how we are going to connect with his presence, to wherever he is currently being held. Once you hold onto that, I might be able to connect you spiritually to his location."

"Is this going to be painful for them?" Cole asked.

Leighton replied sarcastically. "If we are going to play twenty questions, this isn't going to work," she shot back.

I was immediately annoyed and started to speak up when Daxon shot me a "don't even think about it" glare, so I bit my tongue.

"Once you have that interaction in your mind, I need you to close your eyes and visualize yourself there."

I thought about the conversation with my father in the training room. I concentrated on the emotions I had and closed my eyes, just as Leighton asked. As I did, I felt her hand grab one of mine, and I suspected that her other hand went to Daxon's. The second all of us were connected, it felt as if an electromagnetic shock went through my soul. All of a sudden, I was hurled into another realm.

When I opened my eyes, I was in a dark, concrete room that smelled of mildew and mold. It was colder than a winter day, and when I blew out a sigh, I saw my breath.

"Daxon!" I yelled, but there was no response. Wherever I was, I was here alone. Walking with my hands out in front of me, a thin line of light coming through the crack in the concrete grabbed my attention, and I walked toward it, like a moth to the flame.

I made my way to the crack, hearing the hush of murmured voices. One distinctly sounded familiar. Gareth. My curiosity piqued, and I went to the voice. I shifted my body and made my way through the opening, and I was now face to face with what looked like a row of tombs. Gareth was present as was another individual whose back was to me, blocking whoever they stood in front of.

"Tell me again where the gemstone is," the hooded man asked, and there was a whisper from the victim sitting in front of him. "That's all you get. One more time or this isn't going to end well for you." The victim remained admirable, and he responded with silence.

"Very well, it's your life," he said, raising a blade to plunge into the victim. As he descended downward, he shifted slightly to the left. I was brought face to face with the image of my severely beaten father.

"NO!" I screamed, and the vision went black.

THIRTY-FOUR

COLE

What the fuck is happening?" I snarled to the seer as Henny was in a trance-like state with her eyes locked shut. Her head rested on her chest, she was whimpering, but her body was rigid. When I bent down closer, a sheen of sweat was on her brow and blood was dripping from her nose. My wolf snarled at the danger my mate was in. "Get her the fuck out of this!" I screamed as I came face to face with the seer.

She looked up at me, never breaking contact with Henny or Daxon's hand. "It's not that simple, breaking the vision before it's over can cause subconscious damage. Individuals need to come out of it themselves once they are brought in."

I looked over at Daxon, who remained unaffected by the connection; however, his eyes were still closed, and he was also in a trance. "Why does she sound like she is in pain? He seems fine," I said with urgency.

"If the visionary is sensing pain in the vision, that can equate to physical pain in this realm," Leighton responded with weariness in her eyes. It appeared she was starting to get as unsettled with this as I was.

Daxon started stirring, but Henny still remained frozen as the bleeding increased from both of her nostrils.

In a statement of panic, I knelt before, her trying to coax her out of it. Grabbing both of her cheeks in my hands, I put my forehead to her temple trying to will my strength into her body. "Henny, come on. Wake up," I whispered, praying to anyone who would listen that she could hear me. As if upon request, movement started in her limbs, and I was startled by her actions.

"NO!" she screamed as her body was launched from the chair to the floor. I tried to catch her, but her back landed on the ground of the darkened room. I grabbed her body, taking in her unconscious form, and alarm shot through me. I tried once again to rouse her with my plea.

"Henny, come on baby, wake up. I need you to wake up for me," I repeated. As she took in a breath, it felt like oxygen was being released back into my own body and my muscles sighed in relief. I was so consumed with Henny, I didn't even realize that Daxon, Leighton, and Bran were all standing behind my crouched form when she came to. Her eyes opened, and I was met with the beautiful, blush-colored irises that I have grown to love. As if catching her mistake, she blinked again and the blue returned.

"Oh, thank fuck," I said as I blew out a sigh of relief, pulling Henny up into my arms for a hug, only she pushed me away with fear in her eyes.

"I know where my dad is. We have to go now," she exclaimed, trying to climb to her feet as all of us were sensing her panic.

We rushed to make our way upstairs, and Henny suddenly stopped and turned toward Leighton. "Thank you," she said. "We'll never forget that you did this for us," Henny offered.

"Of course. It's fine, now go!" Leighton exclaimed as we dashed the rest of the way up the steps to the top floor of Turner's. Thankfully, Bran and I had driven, so we all hopped into the Ram as we took off.

"He's at Saint Louis Cemetery," she said with urgency.

Daxon was getting ahold of the other hunters, sharing our location with them. "Alright, I let everyone know the plan," he said. "We're going to have to make a stop for weapons. If that is where my dad is being kept, you'd better believe he's not being watched by a few newborn vampires. Hang a right up here at the corner. Everyone is going to meet us at a checkpoint just outside of the cemetery." Bran and I made eye contact, and I nodded giving a silent reply to Daxon's request. Henny went into the details of her vision.

"Gemstones? What gemstones?" Bran questioned as his confusion masked my own.

"I'm trying to think of what they were talking about, but I can't think of anything. But no matter what it is, apparently, it's a life or death matter," Daxon said.

"It's the prophecy. It all comes back to the prophecy," Henny said as Daxon looked at her questioningly. "Didn't you pay attention to Dad when he used to talk to us about this, ever?" she inquired. Daxon only shrugged his shoulders, so she continued. "The elements, Dax," Henny responded flatly. "The elemental gemstones."

"What do the gemstones have to do with the prophecy?" Bran asked as he continued down the deserted road, making his way to the spot Daxon had navigated.

"No, I remember now," Daxon said. "Think of it as a failsafe. In order for the true heir to righteously reign, she not only has to have the ability to yield the four elements, but she also has to have the elemental gemstones in order to yield the magic in its highest form."

I turned around in the passenger seat, trying to comprehend this new information. "Let me guess," I countered. "There is a gemstone for each element?"

It was Henny who answered. "With a fifth and final gemstone to connect them all," she replied as she played with the diamond pendant that she wore around her neck. A diamond that I have never seen her take off. A diamond pendant that now blazed with significance. As if reading my reaction, Henny released her necklace and tucked it back into her shirt.

"Where are the gemstones?" I asked.

"That's where it gets complicated. In order for them not to fall into the hands of the wrong individuals, they are scattered across the different realms."

I cursed at Daxon's statement. Different realms? How the fuck were we going to find those?

"That's a different story for another day," Daxon replied. "We're almost to the safe house. Thankfully, this is one that we have kept off the radar for this exact reason. Only Henny, Dad, and I know about it."

Henny and I locked eyes in the mirror, and I could read the fear in them. "We're going to get to him," I said. Only Henny looked as if she hadn't believed me.

"They will kill him," Henny responded as the car grew silent.

We pulled up to the safehouse. Henny and Daxon shot out and went right into the tiny hut that sat on the outskirts of the warehouse district. Bran and I stayed in the car when he turned his attention to me.

"Cole, this is so fucked up," he said, as serious as I'd ever seen him.

"I know," I responded. "But I have to save them, I have to save her."

"Then lets fucking do this," Bran replied.

THIRTY-FIVE

HENNY

Exiting Cole's truck, I bounded into the hut that housed weapons we stored in case of an emergency. I was completely rattled and shaken by the vision Leighton's magic produced. The chill from the concrete tomb, the darkness from the shadows, the haunted look on my father's face, it all felt so incredibly real. Along with my father's, I couldn't stop thinking of the smug look Gareth held. The animosity from his deception resonated just as highly as my need to rescue my father. The second that he was safe, I was going to rip Gareth, and whoever he was working with, to shreds.

I had to blink back the tears that were ready to emerge from my overflow of emotions. I held back, though, I would use those emotions to fight for my family. Pulling handguns and daggers from the floorboards, I'd tucked them around my body, sliding knives into their holsters. I pulled out a crossbow, admiring the strength of the weapon. The satisfying thought of sending an arrow directly into my father's abductor flashed in my mind, but I set the crossbow aside. That was Daxon's specialty.

"Are you going to save anything for me?" I heard Daxon call from the doorway he leaned against, and I gestured to the crossbow that now sat beside me. He gave a small half smile as he walked over, also admiring the quality of the bow. Kneeling in front of me, he directed my attention to him. There was a mask of concern on his face.

"Are you okay?" he rasped as if feeling my pain in this moment. With our twin connection, it was quite possible he perceived my emotions.

"This is all my fault. You understand that, right? If I wasn't a product of the prophecy, he would have never been targeted. It should have been me." I said, biting back a fresh wave of tears. I blinked and turned away, the last thing I was going to do was cry in front of my brother.

"Hey," he replied, grabbing my forearm. "This is not your fault, and Dad wouldn't have done anything differently. Don't do this to yourself. My sister is not a woman to revel in guilt and anguish. My sister is the badass who, if someone hurts her, she kicks ass and takes names. Do you understand?"

Daxon's words of encouragement, albeit brief, resonated a spark within me. I nodded and stood with a newfound sense of conviction. I strapped a final weapon to my back—a sword. Gareth had a whole world of hurt coming for him.

"Oh, and when this is all said and done, we need to talk about the werewolf," he said as he stood, tucking the crossbow under his arm.

I scrunched my nose not wanting to think about talking about Cole with Daxon.

"What I saw down in that basement, when you were laying there unconscious, wasn't the look of a man who was looking for a fling. It was the look of a man who thought his whole world was crashing down around him. I don't think you've been completely honest with me."

I shuffled back and forth anticipating the amount of information I wanted to share at this moment. *Is this really the time for this?* The defiant look on his face let me know that he wasn't going to drop the subject, and for once in my life, I was at a loss of words. Realization dawned on his face as he gave me an incredulous look.

"You love him," he said, baffled by his own words. A mix of emotions crossed his face.

"Yes," I whispered.

"And does he love you?" Daxon asked, giving me a more pointed look.

"I do," Cole responded as both of our heads snapped toward the door.

Bran peeked at us from behind him, trying to suppress a smile. Daxon made his way over to Cole. Cole seemed completely unfazed that Daxon held a crossbow in his hand. *Ah, yikes.* I shot up and moved as fast as I could to stand between them. Without even realizing it, Cole had shifted me so that I was more behind him than between the two of them. Protecting me as always.

"I don't fucking like it," Daxon snarled through gritted teeth.

Cole chuckled. "Yeah, well, I don't fucking care," he responded.

Panic went through me at what was happening. This situation was the truest definition of the wrong place at the wrong time.

"Daxon," I pleaded. "We have to get to get Dad."

At the mention of our father, Daxon's stance softened a little bit, but his eyes still held the intensity of a raging fire, which was directed at Cole. He stormed to the door, but he stopped to look directly at me.

"We will talk about this later," he choked out. "With Dad," he said as he exited the hut.

I closed my eyes and let out a deep sigh of exhaustion. As always, Bran was the one to lighten the mood.

"Don't worry," he said. "We'll get him to love us soon enough."

I certainly hoped he was right, I thought as we made our way back to the truck.

THIRTY-SIX

COLE

The four of us remained on edge for the remainder of the ride, which was filled with a constricted silence. A general sense of unease began to resonate in my torso as if it were subconsciously anticipating what's to come. The only details we had to go on were the descriptions from Henny's vision. In other words, we were very much traveling into this situation blind. There could be two vampires holding Jonah, or fifty. Bran confirmed that my siblings were on the way as we slowed to a stop outside of the Saint Louis cemetery. I was growing more anxious at my surroundings, and my wolf had started to become unsettled, yearning to be let out.

Upon exiting the vehicle, the fog seemed to thicken. An eerie stillness began to take over as if forecasting a sense of impending doom. Being deep into the middle of the night, we were only met with the sounds of our voices and the company of our shadows. Making our way to the entrance of the cemetery, the street lamp above us flickered before it had burned out completely. Talk about irony. We all were looking at each other with a sense of foreboding.

It didn't take long for my siblings and Henny's hunter province to arrive. The group had made their own stop for weapons. A third car pulled up. I was surprised, but appreciative, to see the Atlanta pack exiting the vehicle. We were going to need all the help we could get.

Walking to meet us where we remained hidden in the shadows, the hunters were stashing their weapons when Henny signaled to them. We now formed a small, half-circle, coming together to discuss a plan.

"What's our play here?" Liam inquired with Lexi nestled into his side. *Always the leader.*

It was Henny who broke the silence. "Long story short, the vision showed me that Gareth and an unknown subject are holding my father captive somewhere in the cemetery. I was so wrapped up in the vision, I couldn't really determine exact markers or distinguishing features. But, if I had to guess, I would say they were stationed in between the catacombs." Henny said. She was in hunter mode now. It was a good look on her.

"So, they could be anywhere?" Liam questioned.

Henny was solemn with her answer. "Yes, they could be anywhere. I think it would be wise if Daxon and I went in first, while everyone else came up the rear and the sides. If we—"

"No," I said flatly. At my statement, six sets of hunter eyes were now staring at me in stunned silence. I shifted my gaze to Liam as he shook his head, informing me that this was neither the time nor place to let my Alpha authority shine through. But I didn't care, my wolf stirred inside me restlessly at the idea of Henny going in without me by her side.

"Excuse me?" Daxon responded. He started to step toward me, still clearly bothered by the events in the safehouse.

"Where she goes, I go. It's that simple," I responded, meeting the challenging flare of his gaze. He may have thought she was his to protect before, but she was mine now.

I felt my heart rate start to quicken. Due to the uncertainty of the situation and my concern over Henny, I was having little control over my ability to keep the Alpha at bay. I could feel my bones start to shift and my eyes were beginning to glow, signifying that I couldn't hold on much longer.

"She is going with me," I snarled, but Daxon didn't back down. As if in slow motion, both the werewolves and the hunters started to surround us. It was only when Henny had stepped in between us that I stopped in my tracks.

"Alright, just listen," she started in a hushed whisper. "You two better get your shit together. There are bigger things at play here then your testosterone fueled argument. I think you're forgetting that I'm a trained hunter who has been doing this almost as long as I could walk. This was my vision, this is my issue, and we are doing this my way. You understand?" Henny said as if challenging anyone to go against her.

Daxon nodded tersely as Henny turned to me. Yeah, I got it, but I didn't like it. I took one more look at Liam for his thoughts on the matter, and he nodded yes once more, indicating that it was the right call. If anyone knew Gareth's ways, it was Henny.

Taking in her beautiful gaze, the attractiveness of her commanding nature, and it only made me want her even more. At that moment, I would give her whatever she wanted. I nodded in agreement.

"As I was saying," she continued to the rest of the group. "Daxon and I will go in first and then break off in two-by-two pairs coming up the sides of the cemetery. This will help us get a better angle if there are groups hiding within the different surroundings. As one group goes, wait five minutes, and then the next group can follow. In the event you're ambushed, just announce your distress because at that point, it's already too late."

"Tate and Nessa, you are on my right. Mason, take Reed to the left. Cole, I trust that you and Landon can best navigate the pairings for your packs?" she questioned as she looked at me, and I nodded.

"Right, I'm hoping that with the two werewolf packs, we'll have the element of surprise," she added as she took a deep breath, looking at those from her province and then back to all of us. "This is nothing that we haven't done before," she said with a slight smile, trying to instill confidence. The others grouped together as Daxon whispered something into Henny's ear, and she nodded.

Ready to go, the hunters got into position, but Henny hesitated, then turned to face me, her blue eyes locking onto mine. It looked as if unspoken words remained on her tongue. She knew the same possibility that I was too scared to vocalize, that one of us might not make it out of this alive.

My stunning and fearless warrior looked as beautiful as ever, and in that moment, it was just her and me as time seemed to stand still. Even though Henny and I recognized what we were to each other, we've never openly acknowledged our relationship in front of anyone else. Sure, my siblings are aware of the mate connection, but together, we've always portrayed a level of distance due to the circumstances of us as a pair.

Eyes still locked with mine, Henny spoke, looking right at me. "It's okay," she said. "It's going to be okay," she declared as she said the words I have spoken to her so many times before. As the light hit her facial features, I detected a glimmer of tears that were threatening to fall. Blinking them back, she gave me one last concerned glance and turned to leave with Daxon. I couldn't help what happened next.

In a few quick steps, I captured her wrist, whirling her around as I crashed my lips to hers. Expressing the same level of urgency, Henny matched my intensity as her lips danced over mine. We both poured so much love into the kiss not knowing the next time we'd be able to do it again.

"Dear sweet Jesus, it's about fucking time!" Bran exclaimed at our first open display of affection. Lifting my eyes from hers momentarily, I took in the diverse emotions of Henny's province. Reed and Nessa beamed while Tate's eyes widened to the size of baseballs. Mason turned a deep shade of scarlet as the vein in his forehead sprouted out of jealously. *That's right, she's fucking mine.* My wolf purred at the proclamation. Daxon balked at the kiss and got back to business. I'd have to work on him.

"Alright, gross. We get it. We need to go," Daxon said, his tone serious.

I turned my attention back to her and pulled her near once more, closing my eyes to rest my forehead against hers.

"I'm right behind you," I whispered, brushing my knuckles across her cheek, burning this moment into my memory.

Henny nodded, pressing one more chaste, but hard kiss on my lips before turning to follow Daxon. I caught one last look at her retreating form before the darkness of the cemetery swallowed her whole.

THIRTY-SEVEN

HENNY

Taking a few steps into the cemetery, I was hit with a sense of dread. An anxiousness came over my body. They were here, I felt it. Lurking in the shadows, they watched us from within.

"Ah, Ladies first?" Daxon pointed.

"Baby," I responded and moved forward.

Making our way further into the cemetery, every creek and shadow became louder than the step before. The hundreds of tombs mocked us as they cast shadows of all different shapes and sizes. Everywhere we turned, it looked like someone was there. Coming up to the first intersection, I knew where we had to go.

"To the right," I said.

"You sure?" Daxon asked, and I nodded again.

"I feel it," I replied as another chill crept down my body.

By this time, the others should be slowly making their way into the cemetery. I was taking the silence as good news because if something happened, we would hear. As we walked, an orange glow at the end of the row became apparent, and the scene from my vision formed. My breathing quickened at the mirrored image in front of me. Daxon and I locked eyes, and he understood what was happening.

We slowed to a creep and drew our weapons. We rounded the corner, going to the entrance of the catacombs. What I saw in front of me stopped me dead in my tracks.

In the middle of a small circle of grass, my father kneeled. He was bound and gagged into silence. His badly beaten eyes fluttered up and connected with mine. Horror took over his gaze, warning us off.

"NO!" I screamed as I did in my vision and raced to my father, but Daxon caught me from behind. Thank God he did, because Gareth rounded the corner and stood next to Dad.

"Amazing," Gareth responded. "Just as we predicted, the two Bradford saviors would swoop in and save the day." Placing his hands behind his back, Gareth took a cocky stance as a smug smile floated across his face. A smile that I would end momentarily. Daxon slowly let go of me, shifting so we were side by side, readying our weapons.

"You're a piece of trash, Gareth," I seethed, but his smile only widened.

For the first time since the warehouse, I took in his form. Gareth had always been one of our fiercest warriors; however, the current movement of his muscles and the tension coiled in his limbs was tighter than normal. He even stood taller, broader than I noticed last time, and his skin held a pasty glow. He grinned a little larger, acknowledging my realization. As he turned, the moonlight flashed on his perfectly white, razor-sharp teeth.

"They turned you," I uttered.

Daxon's eyes went from mine to Gareth's as he stood in a state of shock.

"Smart girl," he remarked. "Although, you always were the smartest, the quickest, and the most reckless," he said as he rolled his eyes. "The number of times I had to come in to save you was tiring. I had grown bored, doing the same thing day after day after day, until one day, I was shown what real authority looks like."

"You see," he continued walking a crescent shape around my father. "We were hunters. We're agile, quick, trained to execute battle in an illicit manner, but in the end, compared to all supernatural creatures, we were the easiest to kill. How strong could we possibly be? Now having those skills all while being immortal? That's real power."

"Gareth, you sick fuck," Daxon gritted out as he took a step toward him.

It was my turn to stop him this time. I needed Gareth to confirm one suspicion before we took him out.

"The other hunters, you're changing them, aren't you?" I asked.

Daxon was stunned. "You're creating more like you?"

A sly smile came over Gareth's face. "Ah, ah, ah, that's none of your business."

"The missing girls?" I inquired, trying one last time.

Gareth cocked his head to the side as if laughing at his own personal joke. "I think you already know the answer to that."

I felt a buzzing around me, and the air changed. It seemed like time slowed down, granting me the ability to sense what would happen next. *To the right.* Having an advanced warning, I turned to see the vampire coming at me before it happened. In an instant, I pulled the sword from the strap on my back and swiped so hard that I almost slashed his head clean off his shoulders. As that happened, time accelerated to normal speed, and pandemonium followed.

Vampires descended upon us from all angles. Automatically, Daxon turned so we were back to back and could defend each other as we have done so many times before. With swift movements, Daxon loaded two bolts into the crossbow, sending them flying at two vampires, the wooden steaks soared through their chests with expert precision.

I was about to face two vampires of my own when I heard similar sounds of battle in the distance. My dread increased, knowing that the rest of my province was out there, that *he* was out there, and they were most likely experiencing the same fate as I. Trying to stay alive, I slid on my right knee, bringing my left leg up, jolting the vampire in the chest, which sent him hurtling backward. Using that momentum, I crouched on the balls of my feet, springing upward to flip over the second vampire, landing directly behind him.

I brought my blade forth, ending the second vampire. The vampire I kicked in the chest made his way to me when an arrow sailed through his chest. Nodding my gratitude to Daxon, I locked eyes with Gareth, who exhibited uncontrollable rage that we were killing his vampires one by one; that's when I lunged for him.

Gareth was a worthy opponent before, but now with the newfound vampire venom running through his veins, he was almost unmanageable. His speed was unlike anything I had ever encountered, and just as I was about to swipe at him, his counter measure struck me. I landed flat on my back with the wind knocked out of me. I rolled to get up as my father's worried gaze stared back at me. He strained to get out of his bindings to help.

It was my father's last-minute gaze to Gareth that made me look up, narrowly missing his cast-iron fist. I rolled to my left, sliding into a crouch. Capturing a second knife out of my boot, I now held a sword and dagger in each hand. I charged Gareth once more, but he was quicker than before. I swiped right and left, but he dodged both offensive moves, bringing his elbow up the gap, crashing it into the right side of my face. Stars formed before my eyes.

I stumbled before regaining my composure, but he hit me one more time, causing a new level of disorientation. I dropped to my knees as my eyes slid over to Daxon, who fought off two more vampires. Even though it looked like he was outnumbered, he held his own. *Thank God.*

I was taken out of my reprieve when a mountainous hand gripped my neck and lifted me off the ground. I clawed at the hand as I battled for air. I heard Daxon scream my name in the distance, but the illusion from my injury made it sound like he was under water.

"You see, Henny," Gareth said as my eyes slid lazily over to his.

He continued to deplete the oxygen from my system. I tried to balance on my toes, but he lifted me higher and higher off the ground.

"Hunters are no match for this new breed of vampire, even the ever-perfect champions, Henny and Daxon Bradford. I will truly enjoy ending you," Gareth sneered.

This is it. This is how I die. Of all the stupid shit I've done, and this is how it's going to end? I've thought this before, I thought this the night it all began.

Clasping both of my hands on his in an attempt to loosen his grip, I tried garnering any element that would come to me, but my strength was too far depleted. I couldn't achieve the jolt I needed. The more I tried to bring the powers forward, the more my vision darkened around my eyes. I temped one last look at my father, who sat helplessly, his eyes glistening with tears. I sent him a silent *I love you* as I accepted my fate.

I closed my eyes and pictured the first time I viewed the blazing green eyes I have come to love so much. I imagined the feel of his touch, but I was ripped away from the memory as Gareth was taken down to the ground by a tremendously colossal werewolf, who now stood protectively in front of me. I gasped at the air reentering my lungs. Rolling into a crouch, Gareth let out a hiss as the werewolf heightened himself on all fours, almost coming eye level with Gareth.

The wolf in front of me had the deepest cocoa colored fur, with dagger-like teeth snarling in fury as he growled. The fierceness of the sound was comparable to a freight train. Looking up, I caught a gleam of smoldering green eyes. *Cole.* My heart shuddered with relief.

Taking in his intimidating appearance, I wasn't prepared for the prominent size of Cole's form. I noticed two more wolves flanking either side of me. Their attention was pulled away from me as more vampires came out of the shadows. Cole and Gareth circled each other as I tried to gain the power to stand.

Gareth, seemingly confident that his newfound vampire abilities were stronger than the Alpha werewolf in front of him, launched himself at Cole. Cole met his intensity, and they collided midair.

Daxon, finally ridding himself of his vampires, started in my direction as I still tried to regain my footing. Appearing behind him, as if in slow motion, a strong hooded figure slithered from the other side of the catacombs. His face was completely hidden by the cloak that hung from his body, but magic radiated off his façade. The only visible part of him was his hands, which were covered in ancient markings. I barely got a look before he clenched and unclenched his fists, continuing toward us.

I mustered up what strength I had to scream a warning to my brother. Daxon turned to meet the sorcerer, who was preparing to attack. Daxon lunged but was rooted to his spot and his weapons dropped to his side, and he gripped his head in agony, the pain causing him to fall to the gravel. As the sorcerer raised his hands higher, Daxon succumbed even further as his right arm cracked, breaking instantly. Through blurred vision, I tried to make my way to him. Gareth and Cole were still going head to head, and Liam and Bran were fighting vampires of their own. Daxon's screams were enough to break me out of whatever pain-filled reprieve I was in, and I mustered the magic forward. Using every ounce of energy that I had, I called the elements, praying that I would have enough strength to circulate the power I had kept buried for so long.

Trying to repeat the movements of the night I saved Cole, I willed fire forward, but the magic remained unmoving. I closed my eyes, taking a deep breath while searching further into my soul. I felt a more ancient power take over.

Whereas before, I felt liquid fire moving through my veins, ice now filled my appendages, frost flowing through my vessels at an alarming speed. The sorcerer was only a breath away from Daxon, and my body automatically reacted. My hands launched a vigorous stream of water that turned into ice midair. My new aqua weapon hurtled toward the sorcerer, but he caught it at the last second. His eyes captured mine in wonder.

"Impossible," he responded as he spoke with awe.

It was just the distraction needed. Out of the corner of my eye, my father, who must have broken free of his binding, charged toward the sorcerer. I launched myself forward to stop him.

In what seemed like slow motion, the sorcerer took the dagger of ice and stabbed my father in the chest. I almost didn't register what happened until I saw the ice sticking out of him. Unsuspecting of the attack, my father was stopped in his tracks, eyes going wide as the dagger struck a fatal blow. Removing the iced dagger from my father's body, the hooded villain threw it at my feet, as if to taunt me.

"Let this be a message, you are no match for me," he said before he turned on his heel and disappeared into the night. I ran forward to catch my father, who fell forward, screams of anguish filled the air and it was hard to distinguish any sight or sound through the noise. I recognized the haunted shrieks as my own. My mind registered what happened. Turning him as we both fell to the ground, my father looked up at me with pride as he struggled to take his final breaths. I tried forcing as much pressure onto the wound as I could with the palm of my hand, but the blood only flowed faster and faster.

"It's okay," I sobbed. "It's going to be okay. Daxon!" I screamed, not even checking to see the status of my brother's safety. With whatever force he had left, my father lifted his hand to my cheek and wiped away the tears that now fell freely down my face. He had a contented smile on his face.

"You look just like her," he murmured, now upon his final breaths. "Remember, you are the key," he stated, but he was not making sense. "I love you both so much." His declaration of love was the last statement my father spoke as his head fell to the side, the light escaping through his eyes. Laying my father down gently, I rested my head on his chest as the sobs tore through me.

"Oh God, what I have done?" I whispered, comprehending the gravity of the situation. If it hadn't been for the inability to control my powers, this never would have happened.

Racked with an unattainable amount of grief, I couldn't control the amount of pained energy that flowed through my body. Rage mounted inside me for the man that ended my father's life. It was with this dire emotion that heat flooded my body and my skin burned. Flames flickered from my fingers at an uncontrollable capacity. The ground rumbled as thick vines broke the surface of the ground, while the wind picked up speed. Letting out a final scream of agony, the flames grew as my emotions intensified. Looking up to the horrified faces of the werewolves, vampires, and hunters, the last thing I saw was glowing green eyes before I cast the entire world around me in fire and ice.

EPILOGUE

It was a warm, breezy night in the land of the Fae. The sprites playfully danced their way around the wooded area as the sounds of the crashing waves created a soothing rhythm from mother nature. Vivid shades of orange and red painted the sky as the sun finally set, bringing a sense of calm to end the day. Olin dipped his hands into the water and washed them gently before he made his way back home for the evening.

As he stood, a shock rippled through his system, and his skin burned where images scorched themselves onto his forearm. As the symbols appeared, he recognized their significance instantaneously: earth, wind, fire, and water. He knew the meaning of the emblems and rushed home.

Olin made it back to his quiet residence deep in the wooded realm. The door opened quickly as Celeste's concerned face stood there sensing his presence.

"Darling, what is it?" she asked, her face full of concern.

Olin rolled his left sleeve up to his elbow and showed her the images burned onto his skin. A gasp escaped her mouth as her soft, delicate hands covered her face.

Olin nodded, confirming her realization.

"It has begun."

ACKNOWLEDGMENTS

Joe: Thank you so much for being such an amazing husband and partner throughout this journey. From walking me through ideas, to encouraging me and giving me strength, I don't know what I would do without you. Thank you for being supportive through endless nights of writing. I love you!

Jane: Thank you SO much for everything you have done for me! You were an amazing editor and I am so appreciative of all the guidance you have given me. As a new author, I am so grateful for your help navigating this process. Thank you!

Justin: Thank you so much for all of your hard and amazing work on the cover! It truly means a lot to me!

Rose, Kristen, and Jennifer: Thank you so much for reading my story! Your tips, thoughts and comments were truly helpful and I appreciate your help!

Melissa: Thank you so much for such a gorgeous interior!

My family and best friends: Thank you for cheering me on along the way no matter how I was feeling. Your encouragement has helped me soar. I love you all!

ABOUT THE AUTHOR

B.K. Rae graduated from Western Michigan University with a BS in Health Services and a MS in Administration from Central Michigan University. B.K. Rae currently lives in Detroit, Michigan with her husband, two kids, and her two adorably goofy Labrador Retrievers. A Hunter's Fate is B.K. Rae's debut novel and the first installment in the Supernatural Province Series. When not writing, she enjoys spending time with her husband and kids, traveling, and reading all things Paranormal Romance and Urban Fantasy.

Made in the USA
Middletown, DE
16 November 2019

78548732R00128